MW01519556

sprinkle all the way

EVERGREEN LAKE: UNDER THE MISTLETOE

KAYLA MARTIN

Miranda,

Happy reading! ♥

[signature]

Sprinkle All the Way

Evergreen Lake: Under the Mistletoe (#2)

Kayla Martin

To the tattooed employee I saw at Crumbl Cookie once, thanks for this.

"You see, turtle doves are a symbol of friendship and love. And as long as each of you has your turtle dove, you'll be friends forever."

-Home Alone 2: Lost in New York (1992)

Dear Reader,

Please be aware that this story contains multiple open door romance scenes that have on-page consensual sexual intimacy. If you are interested in knowing which chapters these scenes happen during you can visit the Dicktionary before the acknowledgments.

This story covers the following topics: mentions of parent death (past) and strained parent relationships. I hope I have done these topics justice based on my own experiences and through the guidance of my alpha and beta readers. As always, your mental health is the most important thing, please take care of yourself first before anything.

All my best,

Kayla

playlist

The songs on this playlist represent the overall story and vibes of *Sprinkle All the Way*. If you enjoy book playlists you can find it on Spotify by searching "Sprinkle All the Way"

Main Title "Somewhere in My Memory" (From "Home Alone") by John Williams

Guilty as Sin? by Taylor Swift

imgonnagetyouback by Taylor Swift

Santa Tell Me by Ariana Grande

Please Notice by Christian Leave

Friendship? by Jordy Searcy

santa doesn't know you like i do by Sabrina Carpenter

"Do You Wanna Be Friends?" by Leanna Firestone

All We Ever Do Is Talk by Del Water Gap

Ruin The Friendship by Demi Lovato

A Nonsense Christmas by Sabrina Carpenter

No Control by Dylan Reynolds

All I Want for Christmas Is You by Mariah Carey

So High School by Taylor Swift

Underneath the Tree by Kelly Clarkson

CHRISTMAS TRAIN

WINTER TREE FARM

ICE SKATING RINK

LIPS & HIPS

EVERGREEN ROAD

SIPS ON MAIN

READ BETWEEN
THE WINES

TOWN
SQUARE

GINGERBREADS

MAIN STREET

NADINE'S
NURSERY

POLICE STATION

CHAMBER OF
COMMERCE

HANSON'S
MERCANTILE

FIRE DEPT.

LIBRARY

FAIR ROAD

MECHANIC

CHURCH

WELCOME TO
Evergreen
LAKE

SKI LODGE
THIS WAY

FOR SALE

EVERGREEN LAKE INN

LAKE STREET

**SANTA'S
CLOSET**

**EVERGREEN
PET RESCUE**

**POWDER
ROOM**

THE REINDEER HOLE

LAKE SHORE DRIVE

EVERGREEN
LAKE

**CHRISTMAS
FESTIVAL**

one

VIOLET

SLAMMING THE BRAKES, my car skids to a stop in the snow before I manage to kill someone on my first day back in my hometown since last year.

"Violet, what happened? Are you hurt?" My sister's concerned voice echoes through the car's Bluetooth.

"I'm fine, but I almost hit Bernice," I tell her, my heart still pounding as I wave at one of my hometown's main busybodies as she walks across the street scowling at me with her gray hair poking out of an obnoxiously festive winter hat. Normally, I'm not the most confident driver. But driving through my hometown always stirs up feelings of the one that got away, no matter how long it's been. "I thought I saw something—someone—and got distracted. Do you remember Noah?"

"Boy-next-door-who-would-sneak-into-your-room-Noah? Yeah I remember him."

I can practically see her eyes roll through the phone. I don't know why I'm asking her if she remembers him when I spent most of my teens talking about him. Even with our seven year age difference, Iris was always the one I would go to when I needed advice about him.

"Well I didn't see him, I don't think. I'm not sure what I saw. Anyway, it couldn't have been him because he said he's never coming back here," I tell my sister, repeating something he always said and trying to convince myself my mind was playing tricks on me. The possibility of seeing him while driving through these familiar roads increases my anxiety by the second. The Band-Aid on my finger sticks to the inside of my glove, constantly drawing my attention back to it, and it makes me want to scream. There's too much happening and I don't have time to think about Noah. With the way things ended between us, I'm not sure if I would hit him if I saw him or grab him and never let him go again.

"You left too," Iris chastises me. She's not wrong. I went away to college like he did. But I returned for birthdays and some holidays and nothing more, instead resorting to FaceTime for our primary method of communication. Mom and Iris have been attempting to convince me to move back for years, but I was comfortable in the job and relationship I had outside of this town. Now my car is full of my belongings and I'm home for a Thanksgiving I was supposed to be spending somewhere else. "Speaking of, are you almost at Mom's?"

"Almost. I'm driving down Main Street," I tell her, slowing down to make sure I don't almost hit any more cherished elderly neighbors. I can only imagine what the town gossips would say if I hit someone my first day back, let alone one of their own group.

"Okay, see you soon," Iris says, disconnecting our call. Driving as Christmas music from the local radio station fills the car, I soak in the sights of Main Street, and waves of nostalgia wash over me like I never left.

Evergreen Lake has always been a special place. Best known for our Christmas Festival, the town doesn't hold back when it comes to decorating or activities each year. All of the shops on

Main Street have lights strung across their rooftops, creating a beautiful glow against the snow. By the time I was looking at colleges, I had grown sick of all the Christmas cheer and needed a fresh start.

Moving to San Francisco was the best I could come up with, since I still wanted to be less than a day's drive from home in case anything happened where I was needed, but I never was. When I got there, making friends, finding a job, and eventually meeting Greg all came easily, like that was where I truly belonged. I assumed I would marry Greg and my life would fall into a perfect picture, but he had other plans.

After eight years away, time has finally pushed me back to this town—indefinitely. My mom practically cried when I called her and told her I would be coming home for Thanksgiving. She didn't ask why I was coming home when I had told her I was spending Thanksgiving with Greg's family last month, or why I didn't mention him. I'm sure I'll get interrogated within the first hour of stepping into the house.

Turning onto my parents' street, my stomach is in knots. There's a bit of doubt that creeps to the forefront of my mind as my tires pack the snow beneath them. What if I don't belong here anymore? What if it was too childish for me to be here? Greg was always making comments about how tacky the town was and how many people stayed there beyond high school. But Greg isn't here, and his opinion no longer matters to me.

Shaking the doubt off, I put the car into park and stare at the house. It's like traveling back in time. The driveway is perfectly shoveled thanks to Dad, and Mom's favorite blow up penguin sits in the front yard, the years of wear and tear evident on its duct taped fins. Iris's old Subaru sits parked next to Dad's truck, now equipped with a small stick figure family in the rear window. According to Mom, Iris's optometry office—aptly named using our last name and becoming Emerson's Eyes—is doing well so I'm not sure why she still drives the old thing when she could get a new one.

Leaving most of my stuff in the car, I hop out and tell myself not to glance over at Noah's house. I immediately fail and stare at the house next door. There's only one car in the unshoveled driveway and the only decoration is a wreath on the door.

I recognize the car as Noah's mom's, and I know she's still living there since my mom has kept me updated on all the town gossip. I've heard all about her fairly new boyfriend after Noah's father passed away while we were in college, but I still hope she isn't too lonely with Noah gone somewhere. I was happy when I heard she had a new boyfriend—Noah's parents were never a good match, always fighting and making him feel unwanted.

Before I can linger too long on the past, I hear screaming coming from the front door.

"Aunt Vi!" my five-year-old niece screams as she comes barreling toward me.

"Ava, your shoes and coat—it's cold," Iris shouts from the porch, shoes and jacket in her arms.

Ava doesn't listen to her mother's warning, running full speed in her fuzzy red socks. I drop my purse and open my arms wide right in time for her to crash into me. I spin her and hold her tight, inhaling her cookies and Christmas scent.

"I missed you, lovebug. Aren't you cold?" I ask her, glancing at Iris on the porch. Her eye roll says she's mad, but her smile gives away how happy she really is.

"No. Do you want to build a snowman?" Ava asks, pointing to the snowy front yard and leaning forward so far she almost falls out of my arms. She takes after me when it comes to her clumsiness.

"How about later? I need to say hi to your mom and gram first," I say as she flops over in my arms like a dead fish. I stumble backward to keep both of us from falling on the driveway before scooping up my discarded purse.

She hangs in my arms, her long brown hair bouncing as I walk us toward the house. Iris tosses the shoes and coat through the open door, pulling me into a tight squeeze.

Ava still plays dead in my arms but squeals as she's crushed between me and my sister.

"It's good to have you home," Iris says into my ear. Pulling away, she takes her daughter into her arms. "Should we grab any boxes?"

"Not yet, I need to eat whatever I smell," I tell her. The same smell of cookies clinging to my niece floats out the front door and up my nostrils. Pure sugar and vanilla, one of my favorite scents.

Mention of cookies brings Ava to life. "Cookie time!" she shouts, springing out of her mom's arms and into the house. When she turns the corner toward the kitchen there's a loud crash and I can see her feet sticking out around the corner.

"For fuck's sake," Iris quietly mumbles. "You okay sweetie?" she adds toward the kitchen.

Ava shouts something unintelligible before her feet are gone again. We follow her path to the kitchen, where my mom has a whole cookie factory setup.

"Violet! You're here," my mom shouts, throwing her oven mitt covered hands in the air.

Seeing her standing there, covered in flour like when we used to bake together, I realize how much I need my mom. I rush over to her, wrapping my arms around her and holding on like she might disappear if I let go. Water gathers at the corner of my eyes, one second from escaping as her arms hold me tight.

"Iris, get your sister a glass of water," Mom says, my eyes shut tight to keep the tears in. I hear my sister going through the motions of opening the cabinet and the fridge. The sounds are so familiar they bring me back to being a kid wrapped in my mom's arm crying about the boy next door. Mom moves me toward the kitchen island until my butt hits one of the stools. She breaks the hug and guides me into the seat, removing her oven mitts and cupping my face in her hands.

"Hi, Mom," I finally say, opening my eyes to see hers are watery too.

"Hi, Vi. Drink this," she tells me, taking the glass from Iris. "Then tell me what the hell you are doing here when you're supposed to be with Greg." His name comes out like it's sour to her—she's never told me she doesn't like him, but I could always tell she wasn't his biggest fan.

"Mom!" Iris shouts.

"Gram said a bad word," Ava screams, and I realize she's in the seat next to me already digging into the cookies.

"Ava, pretend you didn't hear that. Have another cookie." Mom pushes a plate toward her.

"Mom," Iris groans. "Ava, go find your father and grandpa and tell them to get Aunt Violet's boxes from the car, please."

"Aye aye," Ava says, hopping down from the stool and running away with her hands full of cookies.

"Jacob's here?" I ask through a sip of water since I didn't see him when I got here.

"Yeah, he's in the other room doing his daily Duolingo with Dad." Iris gestures toward the direction Ava disappeared to. "Now tell us the details before the cookie monster returns," she adds, taking the seat next to me.

I expected to be interrogated when I got here, but I thought they would have given me longer to get settled. It looks like we are skipping all the small talk and jumping right into it instead. Rehashing all the details of the last horrible week of my life right now will balance out the happiness I'm experiencing being home, leaving me in a dull middle ground of numbness. But my family aren't ones to wait for the full story, so I'm going to have to relent to a shorter version of events to appease them for now. How do I tell them my boyfriend broke up with me and asked me to move out right after my job decided they were downsizing and letting me go?

"Greg and I broke up," I tell them.

"That bastard," my mom says without a hint of remorse.

Followed by "I never liked him," from Iris.

"What happened?" Mom asks.

"I don't know. I came home one day last week and he was done. He said he wasn't in love anymore. He had already started packing my stuff, and he informed me since my name wasn't on the lease I needed to move out. And, I quote, 'I wanted to do it before the holidays so you weren't in any more photos,'" I say, with finger quotes in the air accompanied by an eye roll.

"What an asshole," Iris grumbles.

"Mommy said a bad word," Ava shouts from behind us.

"There's a present hidden in the living room. If you can find it you can open it." Iris spins and points toward the living room.

Ava's eyes widen as she darts out of the kitchen.

"Is there really a present hidden?" I ask.

"Guess we'll see if she finds anything," Iris says, popping a cookie in her mouth before mumbling. "Continue."

"That's pretty much it, although he was getting awfully close to his coworker—Amber—so I can't say I was surprised. At least he left for his mom's earlier this week so I was able to pack all of my stuff in peace." I finish my water and avoid making eye contact with them.

"I'm so sorry sweetie," my mom says, wrapping her arms around my head and pulling me toward her.

"Wait, it gets better," I say sarcastically. "My work also decided they were starting fresh in the new year and decided to get rid of half the project management staff." It's almost funny now that I've had a week to process it, but it still hurts.

"Well fuck," Iris says. "Maybe you need tequila, not water."

Mom's grip on me tightens, her chest rumbling like she's holding laughter in. "They don't deserve you anyway. You can stay here as long as you like. Your room is available, and I also have some boxes for you to go through," she tells me, rubbing my arms.

"Although it's technically their guest room now," Iris adds.

My parents had redone most of the rooms in the house since I've been gone. Everytime I came home for a holiday or birthday they would show me something new. Iris's old room is a home gym, which she says only sees actual activity for the first two weeks of January. While mine has been converted into a guest room. Mom stored all our old things in the basement, and she keeps telling me I need to go through what I want to keep. Now all my new belongings will join the old ones as I figure out what I'm going to do.

"Can I go see it?" I ask, perking up at the excitement. Last year I wasn't able to come home for Christmas since I spent it with Greg's family, and I missed the big reveal.

"Of course, go get settled and come back down. The snicker-doodles are almost done," Mom says, knowing those are my favorite cookies.

We all scatter from the kitchen. Iris goes to find Ava, while I run into Dad and Jacob carrying my boxes in and setting them in the foyer. I hug them and thank them for the help, grabbing my duffle bag full of essentials.

Climbing the stairs, the sixth step creaks like it has since third grade and the feel of the carpet under my feet hasn't changed one bit. I step back on it to hear it again, closing my eyes as I let the sounds of home relax me before continuing.

Old pictures and art we created in school line the halls

upstairs, including all of our school pictures. Iris's are right above mine, and for the first few years we look so similar it's hard to tell who is who. Our wide smiles and brown hair are identical, only our different eye colors give us away. Hers darker, matching her hair, while my blue ones make me look wild with how wide I have them open. As I walk down the line of pictures you can tell when we each went through our awkward phases, braces and glasses making an appearance for both of us. Of course, we've both gotten LASIK thanks to Iris's eye doctor perks. Focusing on mine, I can pinpoint the year Noah moved in next door—it's the year my smile finally reached the corner of my eyes and made them wrinkle.

I notice how much has changed since I've been gone when I open the door to my room. The walls are now a light blue with pictures of snowy mountains. The furniture is all the same, but painted white. My trundle twin bed remains in the corner of the room next to the window, adorned with a navy comforter that looks like it's filled with feathers.

I drop my bag and fall on the bed, needing to test out this new comforter. My landing is just as I imagined, soft and squishy. I can hear the sound of Iris and Ava running around, soft instrumental music filling the house, and the kitchen timer goes off. The weight of life is lighter here, and my confidence that everything is going to be okay slowly increases. I'll figure out where I belong soon.

Running my hand over the soft comforter, my fingers brush over something small and hard to the touch, a stark contrast to the warmth of the comforter. Grabbing it, I realize it's a tube of red lipstick, which must have fallen out of my bag from one of the pockets. I remember being excited about the color, but Greg said it was too bright. He told me I looked like a hooker, and he would be uncomfortable if I wore it. I'm not sure why I ignored that red flag.

Standing, I move to the mirror on the wall. The lipstick is practically brand new as I wipe it across my lips. I look fantastic, my dark hair and blue eyes perfectly compliment the red. Fuck Greg for being insecure and making me self conscious about this color.

Suddenly, the reflection of the house next door through the window catches my attention. The window across from mine is dark, and the blinds are down, but I don't need them up to picture the twin bed against dark green walls covered in horror movie posters. For years I peered into it, seeing Noah climb out to come visit me. My heartbeat picks up at the memory of him spending countless nights in this room with me. Now the window returns nothing but darkness instead of the face I've missed for years, and I can't help wondering where he is now. Probably living the life he always wanted in New York City. I bet he would like this lipstick on me.

two

NOAH

BRAYDEN GIVES me a guilty look as he slides his apron across the counter.

"Not you too," I groan, dropping my head to my hands and rubbing my eyes.

"I'm sorry, man. My mom said if I worked here, I could kiss my new car goodbye," he says, shrugging.

Over the past week, my entire staff has quit on me. Brayden was my last employee, and now I'm left alone. Once word got out I was the one reopening Gingerbreads, people weren't too pleased a delinquent like myself would be running a cookie shop. Teenagers are all I can afford to hire right now, and none of their parents want them working for me. They're acting like I murdered someone, instead they're harboring resentment from the past and making assumptions based on rumors.

"What's the rumor today?" I ask.

Ever since I returned to Evergreen Lake a month ago, everyone equates me being in a situation where someone got arrested to me being in prison. I blame my reputation from high school and record-breaking number of suspensions. I was always getting suspended for starting fights, but I didn't know how else to channel my anger. One particularly bad year at the Christmas Festival another student made a comment to me about my mom and I lost it. I ended up starting a fight that my friends were quick to join in on, which got out of hand and landed me directly in the festival's giant tree. Everyone was less than pleased when it fell over and ruined several stands, including the hot chocolate one. Luckily no one was hurt, but everyone kept their distance from me after that. If anyone knows how to hold a grudge, it's the residents of Evergreen Lake.

That incident landed me my record-breaking suspension number, even though it didn't happen at school. It was the only award I ever won in school—well, an award Violet Emerson crafted for me. A flash of the girl next door fills my mind, her with a smile that reached her bright eyes as she handed me the award. She was so proud of how fast she put it together even though it was just a piece of foil with 'first place' written on it in Sharpie on a string.

The memories are gone as quickly as they appeared and I'm thinking about how this town hates me again. It seems like every day there's a new rumor as to what I did. One day I had supposedly broken into an animal shelter and dyed all the animals key lime green. Nowadays, my dad's voice telling me I'm unwanted is in the forefront of my mind more than ever.

"You drove into a grocery store while trying to use a bong," Brayden informs me, holding in a laugh. He's a good kid, and I was hoping he would be the one employee to stay. But the parents in this place are scary when it comes to getting what they want, especially the moms. And what they want is me gone.

"I don't even smoke," I groan.

"Well, you know how they are. I really am sorry though," he says, running his hands through his shaggy blond hair. He was the first one I hired, so it seems fitting he's the last one standing.

"It's fine, I'll figure something out. If anything changes you're welcome back," I tell him.

"Good luck, man." Brayden shakes my hand before heading out the front door.

Staring at the empty shop, I start to wonder why I returned when I left on purpose years ago. Back to a town that never liked me and full of memories that only leave a sour taste in my mouth—mostly. The only good ones I have of this place either involve a tall brunette or a short old lady, both conjuring drastically different types of memories.

At least one of my old high school friends, Sydney, is back here, too, but that doesn't help my case much. I'm trying to shake off the negative view everyone has on me. Hanging out with the same people from high school doesn't seem like a good idea. Senior year we super glued everyone's lockers shut as part of the senior prank. Sydney and I were the only ones who ended up getting caught for it, and we spent a week cleaning it up. She's been the only one who has treated me like a person since arriving, besides my mom.

With Sydney working next door at Sips—the local coffee shop—I should see more of her, but I've been so busy figuring out this whole small business thing that I haven't had the time.

Even if I did have time, I mostly keep to myself. The shop needed a lot of work when I first got here, and I've been focused on fixing everything. Last New Year's, I expected this year to be full of the same old stuff. Jumping from job to job, hoping I would finally find one I liked enough to stay. I never would have guessed this year would bring me to this town.

The memory of last month comes flashing back, when everything changed after a bar fight that got out of hand. My mom had been trying to call me all night, but I didn't have the energy to answer. By the time I got home it was too late to call her back, so I waited until the next morning. When I finally called her she answered her phone while shopping in Hanson's Mercantile, the local general store.

"*Noah Phillip Callahan.*" *My middle name always made me flinch. One, because it was never good when your mom middle named you. Two, because it was my dad's name, and I tried to think about him as little as possible. I've considered changing it, but I'm too lazy to actually figure out how.* "*I was calling you all last night and you didn't answer once?*"

"*I'm sorry, Mom, I was dealing with something. There was this bar fight and some guys ended up getting arrested so I had to talk to the police,*" *I told her. I also didn't want to call her back, but I wouldn't admit that. I needed a break from her and anything that reminded me of Evergreen Lake. Eight years of a break wasn't enough though—an infinite amount of years wouldn't cut it. No matter what I did, Evergreen Lake was always in the back of my mind with Violet right next to it. I couldn't think about one without thinking about the other.*

"*Well if you had bothered to call me instead of getting yourself arrested, you would know I have some important news for you,*" *she said. I heard the whispers in the background and knew whoever was hearing this conversation was going to spread that misinformation like wildfire. If you wanted the town to know about something all you had to do was speak up in public.*

"*I didn't get arrested, two other guys did,*" *I corrected her.* "*But I know, I'm sorry I didn't pick up.*"

"*Well, either way, you could have sent a text letting me know that you were okay instead of ignoring me. Anyway, you need to come home,*" *she said.*

"*Why? What happened?*" *My heartbeat had picked up, and I needed her to make it fast since I know if we stayed on the phone for too long I would be stuck for an hour hearing about things I didn't* care about. *My mind immediately went to the girl next door, the one thing I wouldn't mind hearing about. She left town when I did, and I never dared to ask about her. Maybe she was back, probably with a rich husband, two point five kids, and a dog. I never hated an imaginary dog so much before.*

"I wanted to tell you this at a better time, but I suppose this will have to do," she said through a sigh. "Sweetie, Ginger died. Her lawyer contacted me looking for you, I think she left you Gingerbreads. Please come home."

Beeping pulls me out of the memory and I rush into the kitchen. I open the oven and pull out the chocolate chip cookies and place them on the counter. The smell of fresh cookies fills the space, and it helps to slow my heart rate.

They look perfect.

I hate them.

There's no point in keeping them since I won't be able to open in December. How can I open with no staff? Why did I think I could open in time for Christmas? One month isn't nearly enough time to fix this place and sort through all the papers in Ginger's office. I thought opening for the beginning of the festival would show the town I care about and want this shop to succeed, but now that all seems futile.

Tossing the cookies into the trash, I turn off the appliances and head upstairs to Ginger's—*my*—apartment.

Falling onto her couch, a defeated sigh fills the silence. I'm sitting here in this apartment alone, and the walls are bare with outlines of old frames from Ginger. My mom and her new boyfriend packed all Ginger's stuff and moved it to the basement before I got here, leaving me with only the furniture and the basics. But it still doesn't feel right.

It's unsettling sitting in her apartment without her here. Ginger was like a grandma to me. Her cookie shop was one of my favorite places to escape to. I never had any money though, and one of the first times I went in Ginger caught me trying to steal a chocolate chip cookie. She didn't react like everyone else though. She let me keep it and told me to come back the next day or she would call my mom.

The next day I showed up and she put me to work. I started on dish duty. When I started asking her questions about baking cookies, she taught me about what she was doing. Soon I was spending my days after school working there or doing homework at one of the small tables with Sydney and our other friends. When I was working I would give them any cookies that were messed up, sometimes messing them up on purpose for my friends. Occasionally Violet would come in, too, and I would sneak her an extra cookie with her order.

It helped to keep me out of some trouble and away from my house. The only thing that pulled me home was the temptation of climbing into the window next door.

Now a box stares at me from the coffee table, filled with sealed letters adorned with instructions on each one. They remind me of all the birthday cards Ginger would send me each year, along with a crisp hundred dollar bill. I've looked through them multiple times, memorizing all the prompts, and I was prepared to open one this weekend. It's sitting on top, mocking me. Just like I never lived up to my dad's expectations, I've failed to accomplish the task Ginger set out for me.

Open the night before you reopen the store

Now I'm unsure when, if ever, I'll be able to open it. There's no way I can run a shop by myself.

Pushing it aside I go for the familiar envelope I've memorized. Picking it up and pulling the letter out I reread the words like there might be something new in them.

Open first

Dear Noah,

I'm sorry to have to do this to you, but you were always my favorite. I've missed you around town. If you're reading this, it means I'm no longer around. A shame, but probably time.

Since I don't have any family I'm leaving everything to you. You have no idea how much I enjoyed it when you worked at Gingerbreads. I loved teaching you, and even if you didn't know it, you were meant to bake. I want to give you an opportunity now.

Move in upstairs, run the shop, and enjoy life.

Hell, sell it if you want. Just don't sell it to some bigshot from the city.

But promise me you'll try to bring the shop back to life. Don't let those town gossips weigh you down. If anyone can do it, it's you.

All my love,
Ginger

P.S. Check under the bed for the recipes – they're taped to the frame

Wiping a tear from my eye, I can't let Ginger down. I don't understand why she thinks I'm the one to run the shop, but she never clued me into her madness. She was always coming up with wild schemes that I questioned until they paid off. Like the time she wanted to bake a peanut butter and jelly cookie, which turned out to be amazing and a best seller for months. It only got taken off the menu after the town moms forced her to remove it because one kid had a peanut allergy.

It's easier said than done brushing off all the people in this town, but I need to find a solution to reopening. I need to have the same confidence in myself that Ginger did. Right now it's like the only thing I can do is fail. I need to prove to this town I'm not the failure they assume I am, and make my dad roll over in his grave.

I glance over at the clock and see it's getting late. I don't think any solutions are going to present themselves tonight. Especially not when I haven't eaten and Thanksgiving is tomorrow. I'm glad I didn't post any signs with an opening date. The windows will have to stay covered in newspaper for a while longer.

Tossing the letter in the box, I put on my boots and jacket and head out the door. I'm not dealing with this right now. Instead, I'm heading to the bar to get a burger and get drunk, even if it means dealing with the potential crowd of old high school classmates home for the holiday.

three

VIOLET

HAVING dinner with my family tonight was the thing I needed most. It's so nice to be home with these people who love me for who I am. I'm starting to realize I never felt loved like I needed with Greg. Being with him was easy because it was predictable, but there was always something missing, like we didn't quite belong together. Then I got so wrapped up in my job that I forgot about it and stopped trying to figure it out, brushing away any doubt of whether we were a good match.

Now I'm free of both the man and the job, and uncertain what the next step is. It's not something my family would understand well, since none of them ever left like I did. My parents have lived in Evergreen Lake their whole lives. They met working at the library as teenagers, and they both still work there.

Iris moved home after school and has been running Emerson's Eyes for a few years now. I was so proud of her when she opened her own practice. She deserves it after all the hard work she's put into getting her degree. Jacob works there with her, working the front desk. He's the perfect match to her stubbornness and ambition. I can't help the jealousy that tightens around my heart at their perfect family.

Everyone has their place here, and I don't know if I fit in. It has always felt like there was something missing here for me. Even in high school, there seemed to be a piece everyone else had and I didn't. I worked with other classmates on the yearbook and the student council, but they always seemed to have plans after school that I never received invites to. The inside jokes and references always went over my head, made at events I hadn't attended. I simply floated from class to class and then home.

Seeing my parents and my sister in loving relationships makes me want to call Greg, which I recognize is a bad idea. He's texted me a few times apologizing, and I can't tell if he wants to get back together or if he's going to ask me where I hid his Xbox controller.

Mom said I could stay here for as long as I wanted, but I don't know if that's what I want. Plenty of my friends live at home, and it's nothing to be ashamed of. For me, overstaying my welcome and moving in here would be a step in the wrong direction.

"Violet, did you want another glass of wine?" Mom's voice breaks me out of my spiraling thoughts.

"Yes, please," I say, passing my empty glass her way. It's only me, Mom, and Iris now. Dad, Jacob, and Ava have moved to the living room to watch sports highlights. I can hear Ava cheering alongside them every now and then, followed by a question of why they're cheering. "Fill me in on the latest town happenings. What's new?" I ask, trying to give myself a distraction.

I think I see a quick glance between my mom and Iris, but I might be making it up.

"We got a stand at the Christmas Festival this year," Iris

tells me. "Hopefully doing some free eye exams will help some of the people in this town realize they need glasses."

"Bernice could probably use some. She walked in front of my car today. I almost hit her," I say through a laugh.

"I wish you would have." Iris rolls her eyes.

"Iris!" Mom yells.

"What? She's a total pain in the ass," she defends her statement, and I nod in agreement.

"Is she still gossiping with Mildred and Sheila?" I ask. The three of them always seemed to know everything about everyone. Thanks to them, everyone in the town knew when I got my period in seventh grade after they saw my mom buying pads at Hanson's. Luckily I was never the target of the mean rumors. I can only imagine what they would have said if they saw Noah climbing through my bedroom window. He wasn't as lucky though. Every time he got suspended, they knew about it. Like they had an inside source in the school office or something.

"It's almost worse this year." Iris rolls her eyes and shares a look with Mom. This time I'm certain I'm not making it up.

"What do you mean?" I inquire, wanting to figure out what they're keeping from me.

"You remember how Ginger passed away, right?" Mom chimes in. I remember how my heart dropped to my stomach, and I had to sit when I heard the news. She was always so kind to everyone who came through her doors, and there wasn't a person in town who disliked her. When I was the class treasurer she would always help host bake sales and fundraisers to help us raise money for the school dances. Mom continues when I nod, "Gingerbreads has been closed since then, and they've spread countless rumors about what's happening to it."

"Typical. Does anyone know who she left it to? She didn't have any family right?" I ask, remembering how she always treated her employees and regulars like her own grandkids.

Noah had always said she felt like a grandma to him, often picking up shifts there to avoid his own family. Part of me wishes I had a way to contact him when I heard the news, to make sure he was doing okay.

"Right. There's no concrete information at this point since there's no signs in the windows," Iris says, avoiding eye contact with me and finishing her glass of wine.

"There's also Jingle Balls." Mom is quick to change the subject from Gingerbreads.

"They still haven't caught them?" I ask, remembering when Iris first told me about the person who kept painting ornaments with caricatures of everyone in the town and hanging them on the festival tree.

"Everyone has their suspicions but there's nothing solid yet. We all hope they'll do it again this year," Iris chimes in. "I'm kind of excited for it. I stole Ava's off the tree last year and kept it."

"Wait, do you have pictures?" I perk up too fast, almost knocking my glass over. My heart aches at how I missed Christmas last year.

"They're on the town's Facebook page, let me find my phone." Mom hops up from the table and runs into the kitchen.

By the time she finds the pictures, we've finished another bottle of wine and I've been filled in on all the latest gossip, new shops, and neighbor updates from the last month. They tell me about how nice Noah's mom's new boyfriend is, and part of me wants to go over to say hi, if only to be closer to Noah again for a moment. But it wouldn't be the same without him there.

"Is there anything else new with you? Besides the jerk wad and your sucky ex-employer?" Iris asks, rolling her eyes.

"That's about it, but I think I'm going to wander and get some fresh air," I say, getting up from the table and taking my glass into the kitchen.

"That's not a bad idea. We should probably get going anyway." Iris stands with me, checking the time on her phone.

I manage to reapply my lipstick and slip out the front door while Iris and Jacob are trying to wrangle Ava, who wants to sleepover at Grandma and Grandpa's house. I need a breather, and the cold winter air of Evergreen Lake is doing the trick.

Walking the snowy streets, I only slip a few times before I realize I might need to get a better pair of winter boots. I wander around for a while before finally ducking into my favorite dive bar.

Stepping into The Reindeer Hole is like stepping into the past. The decor and the people are the same. Joe is still behind the bar, his dark hair now has streaks of gray through it and his eyes have more wrinkles at the corner. Dad always loves to come here after parties have died down at the house for "one quick drink," which never ends up being quick.

As my eyes roam over the full bar I realize this might have been a mistake. I forgot tonight is one of the biggest drinking nights of the year. The bar is packed with people I went to high school with, and I have absolutely zero desire to catch up with any of them. I'm about to head home until my heart stops when I spot the last person I expect to be here.

Noah.

Noah, who lived next door.

Noah, who snuck into my room.

Noah, who moved away and hasn't spoken to me in eight years.

He's sitting at the bar with a beer in his hand, the label half picked off. My body doesn't move as I take in the sight of him, his boyish looks now gone, replaced with more distinguished features. His dark hair is shaggy on top and shorter near his neck. His jawline is as sharp as ever, a dusting of facial hair complementing it.

I consider leaving when I notice his plaid flannel is rolled up to his elbows, and I see his forearms are covered in dark tattoos that stop me in my tracks. Those are a new addition, and one I wouldn't mind finding out more about. Although, there's no way I'll be able to talk to him without saying something stupid. All the memories of him sneaking into my room come flooding back and it's like I've stepped into some weird *Twilight Zone* situation. The world is black and white and the room spins, as if Rod Sterling's voice is about to start an ominous introduction. My stomach twists and I might barf if I don't get out of here soon. Noah makes my decision for me before I can leave when he spins my way and makes eye contact with me.

"Violettttt?!" he slurs as he lifts his beer and stumbles off his stool. I reluctantly push through the crowd and move his way, avoiding the gazes of classmates now directed at me. With his luck he's going to end up slipping and hurting himself. I shouldn't care so much when I haven't seen him in so long. He's the one who abandoned me when we were best friends. He's an adult now, he can take care of himself. But I can't help myself.

I reach him right as he slips, my arms stretching out to keep him steady. "Careful, Noah," I warn him, slipping myself and getting a whiff of the beer on his breath. Historically, he was the one stopping me from falling over and making a fool of myself and it's strange to have that flipped now. His biceps are firm through my gloves and my heartbeat picks up at the contact. The familiarity of him is the same from all those years ago, but the electricity has been increased to the max. My hands want to reach to cool down my cheeks, but I also don't want to let go of him.

"Careful yourself, Vi. If you fall, I fall." His words run together as he lifts his head from our feet to meet my eyes and I have to bite my tongue to keep from gasping. Have his eyes changed shades of green? I swear they used to be a deeper green, but now they seem lighter as he stares at me. I always loved when he would look at me, hopeful and kind. Greg never looked at me the way Noah did. I realize now part of me was always hoping he would one day, and now I'm grateful he never did. Seeing Noah looking at me removes another weight off my chest from the dumpster fire of my life. Without the breakup or job loss, I wouldn't be here touching Noah.

"Someone had to catch you," I tease, dropping my hands from him before I never let go.

He stares at me for a while, and I can't tell if he heard me. We stare at each other as time slows around us. I'm fully aware of the whispers and fingers being pointed our way. They're probably surprised to see me and Noah interacting. After all, we managed to keep our friendship mostly contained to the confines of my bedroom. He was always adamant about not tainting my reputation with his presence, keeping our school lives separate.

He finally speaks after what seems like ten minutes. "Are you real?" He squints his eyes at me and reaches out to touch my hair, picking it up and dropping it in the air.

"Yeah," I laugh, shoving my gloves into my pocket. "I'm real. Do you want to sit down?" I want to talk to him, but I don't want to do it standing in the middle of the bar with everyone watching us. They'll all eavesdrop and report to the town gossips. By morning I'm sure everyone would have the entire transcript to our whole conversation, and I'm unwilling to give them that.

"Of course, this way." He beams and grabs my hand, the skin to skin contact sending a bolt of electricity through my body that I wasn't ready for. My teenage hormones make a reappearance, remembering the dreams I had of him exploring my body. I spent years desperately wishing he would touch me the way I wanted him to, but it never happened. All of our touches were nothing but innocent, two friends simply happy with each other's company and nothing more. But I can't dwell on all the lost time now, not when I have to pay attention so I don't trip as he leads us through the crowd, uncertain how I'm going to survive the rest of this night.

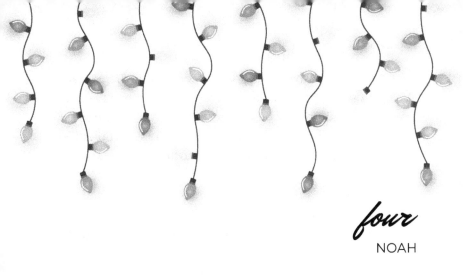

four

NOAH

MAYBE-VIOLET FOLLOWS me to one of the booths against the wall. Sitting on the worn down cushioned surface I stare at the girl across from me. She's no longer next door, but here in front of me. I think. The tingling sensation on my hand from her skin is the only indication I'm not making her up this time.

When I first moved away after graduation I saw her everywhere I went. She was around every corner and in every brunette I interacted with and every laugh I heard. No one ever compared to her though. Her big blue eyes and heart stopping grin always sucked me in and cheered me up when I needed it most. Those lips are now covered in red lipstick, which is a new feature. That probably means she is real, but I still can't be sure. Too many times I've been fooled by dreams that left me panting and hard, but most of all alone.

"Do you still think I'm imaginary?" Violet giggles and my stomach flips. I probably shouldn't have another drink. Her laugh sinks deep into my veins and my body comes alive as the sound travels through me, like it's awakening from a long hibernation.

I nod, unsure what else to say to her after so many years. What do I say to the girl whose image is never far from the forefront of my brain when she unexpectedly shows up in front of me? When she didn't call or text, and now she's all smiles like she didn't drop me like I meant nothing to her?

Nothing.

She rolls her eyes at me as she removes her coat, and the corner of my mouth tips up, remembering all the times she's rolled them before. Her green sweater is one I don't recognize, and I reach across the table to feel it and make sure she's there —the fabric is soft and warm from being inside of her coat. I think I hear her laugh, but when she places her hand over mine I can only focus on the shivers that shoot up my arm and down my spine. I'm no stranger to her touch, but encountering it again after so long is like finding water in the desert. I've imagined this touch on me again, and much less innocently than I care to admit. I want to jump out of this booth and slide in next to her. Crowd her against the wall and whisper things to her no one else in the bar could hear as she gasps my name. Removing my hand from stroking her sweater, she uses her other hand and pinches the back of my hand.

"Ouch!" I shout, pulling away from her and bringing my thoughts back to the fact that she never called.

"Real enough for you?" She lets go of my hand and crosses her arms, giving me a look that tells me I'm being dumb—a look I'm used to from her and one I've missed desperately. I nod before she continues, "My mom said you weren't living at home. I didn't think you were in town."

They're not questions, but statements. I'm too drunk to read between the lines and decipher the tone in her voice. Did her mom not tell her I was home? Is she mad I'm here? Should I not have said hi to her? Should I go home? I bet she's embarrassed to be seen with me. I spent so many years making sure I never ruined her image and now I've destroyed that with one drunken night because I couldn't stay away. There's probably a reason she never called me after I left, and I should have left her alone.

"My mom didn't mention you either," I quip, taking a sip of my beer and falling against the booth. My mom is the queen of dropping Violet into casual conversations. Whether I like it or not, I'm all too aware of how she works at a steady job and comes home for the holidays sometimes. One thing my mom never brings up is whether or not she's involved with anyone and I've always been too scared of the answer to ask.

"Briefly. Some things fell through, so I'm here until the end of the year," she tells me.

"I'm on Main Street," I say, but with my inhibitions lowered, I want to tell her more. Normally I avoid telling people too much about myself, but if there's anyone I could confide in, it's Violet—even if I haven't seen her in years. If she wants me to stop, she'll stop me, but being here with her is the best I've felt all month.

She was always a beacon of comfort for me, and she knows that. Growing up with my parents was never fun. They were the type of couple who shouldn't have ever gotten together. They got pregnant and married at nineteen, a fact my dad never let me forget. When they weren't screaming at each other, he was telling me I was a mistake and how I ruined his life. He was too much of a coward to leave and tried to get out of the marriage by constantly cheating on my mom with his secretaries, and Mom was too stubborn to leave him. Sometimes their fights would end with them throwing things at each other. I have countless memories from childhood of the times I had to pick up shards of glass off the floor when they were done. Sometimes they would make up and it was often louder than when they were fighting. I wanted nothing more than to escape my house.

Moving next door to Violet was a blessing in disguise. I hated having to move the summer before eighth grade and leave all my friends behind. My dad wasted no time pointing her out after her family said hello the day we moved in. The memory of his tight grip on my shoulder as he said, "Don't think about fucking up your life with that girl by screwing her. She'll ruin your life and never let you leave." The thought hadn't crossed my mind until he said it, but after that it was all I could think about.

One night that summer, Violet was in her window when I opened mine to get some air and get my head far away from one of their fights. She asked if I was okay, and there was something in her voice that pushed the truth past my lips. I wasn't. She pointed to the ladder hanging on their shed and told me to come over so I didn't have to listen to my parents.

At first, I went over with every intention to try to get in her pants, because it was the one thing he didn't want me to do. But I also didn't want to give him the satisfaction of knowing I was such a screw up by doing exactly what he expected.

Instead, we stayed up all night talking and I couldn't believe I hadn't spoken to her more before. She listened to me go on and on about how I wanted to finish school and leave for New York City. It always seemed like the place people went in movies to live their life, and that's what I wanted. I also wanted to be far away from my parents.

Both of us trying to fit on her trundle bed was uncomfortable, but it got me away from my house. Eventually she pulled out the second bed, with a mattress far thinner than hers, and I fell asleep listening to her tell me about how she broke her arm jumping off a pool slide when she was six.

Now, I want nothing more than to lie on her bed and catch

her up on the last eight years and hear about everything she's been up to if she is willing to do that.

"Why are you on Main Street?" Violet's voice pulls me back to the present, and the whiplash of my thoughts jumping around has my head spinning.

"You'd never believe me." I shake my head. I still don't believe the situation I'm in.

"This sounds like it's going to take awhile. Let me go grab us some drinks." She goes to stand, but I reach out and stop her. The sudden movement increases the dizziness as I wrap my hand around her arm. My desire to pull her to me and keep her close forever is about to override all rational thoughts.

"I have a tab open, put them on that," I tell her instead. I'd offer to go and get them myself, but I'm unconvinced I'd make it back here. She nods and I watch her push through the crowd to the bar. I can't pull my eyes off her as she says hello to Joe and he runs around the bar to give her a hug. Why didn't I hug her yet? I should hug her soon. Suddenly I'm aware I haven't held her in years and the lack of her leaves a hole in my heart and my arms.

Luckily, she returns a moment later with two beers.

"Okay, tell me everything." She wraps her red lips around the bottle and I have to tell myself not to move to her side.

"You're looking at the proud owner of Gingerbreads," I spit out as fast as I can, lifting my beer and taking a long swig.

Violet chokes on her beer, with some of it slipping out of her mouth and down her chin. It's torture watching her slowly wipe the liquid from her mouth. Her lipstick doesn't budge and it makes me wonder what it would take to mess it up.

"You what?" she splutters once she's cleaned up.

"Ginger left everything to me. Apartment. Shop. Bills," I tell her, lifting one finger for each item and squinting my eyes to focus on her.

"Noah, that's awesome," she shouts, throwing her arms in the air and knocking her beer over. "Shit, my bad."

I reach for the napkins on the table and help her clean up. "It's actually not very awesome," I mumble to myself.

"Wait." She stops wiping and grabs my hand. "Why not?"

This woman needs to stop touching me, or I'm going to tell her about all the feelings I had for her in high school and never acted on. She never showed signs she was interested in me in high school, and that message became crystal clear after she didn't reach out after I left for college. Part of her not reaching out made it easy to stay away for so long. Now that we're both back I'm sure there's no way she would be interested in me now that I'm running Ginger's shop into the ground. My skin burns with each second she keeps her hand on mine. But I also don't want her to ever let go.

"Can't open. Screwed," I confess, shrugging and hiccuping at the same time.

"You need to explain more, I can't keep asking you why." Violet glares at me.

"Too drunk, Vi." She rolls her eyes at me, but waits for me to continue. "No one will work with me, and I can't do it alone. So it's useless," I tell her, and drop my head to the table.

Her delicate fingers are in my hair a second later, scraping along my scalp with nails that are the perfect length. I have to bite my lip so I don't groan like I want to. She always used to give me head massages when I would get too worked up. They'd calm me down, and they even put me to sleep a few times.

"Two steps forward," she says, continuing to rub my head, moving to the spot right above my ear.

"One step back," I echo the second half of the phrase we always said to each other when things got rough. The first time I said it to her was in ninth grade when she failed a test and was nervous about telling her parents. She wasted no time laughing and telling me the phrase was actually "one step forward, two steps back." To which I replied I liked mine better—at least mine was hopeful and got you moving forward. She agreed, and it became one of our many inside jokes.

Tilting my head into her hand as the memory relaxes me, a small groan escapes from my lips without my consent. She instantly pulls her hand away like she's been bitten, and my head pops up.

"What?" I ask.

"Sorry I shouldn't have done that. You don't have a partner or a spouse who would get pissed at me for touching you, right?" Her hands cover her flushed cheeks as she looks around the bar.

"Nope," I reassure her. "What about you?"

"Okay, cool, and no partner for me either. Sorry, I kind of fell into our old habits there," she apologizes, clenching her fists several times before sticking them in her lap.

"Stop apologizing. You know I could stop you if I wanted to," I tell her, and it comes out dirtier than I intended. I can tell she thinks the same thing by the way her mouth forms the smallest 'O'.

"Right, sorry—shit, sorry—shit fuck me," she stumbles through her words before taking a deep breath. "The shop. I'm impressed you're trying to open it, but it sucks you can't."

"Thanks," I take a sip of my beer, entirely uninterested in rehashing my failure and too focused on not mentioning how she said 'fuck me,' which I would gladly do.

"Of course," she says, sitting up straighter. "Now tell me what else is new."

The next few hours go by in a blur as we catch up on inconsequential things about our lives, catching up on eight years of lost time. At one point we try to play darts, but I'm too drunk to aim well, and Violet isn't coordinated enough to aim, period. We talk and laugh until Joe kicks us out.

She tells me she's going to walk me home because I'm still a bit wobbly, and I let her. I'm still skeptical she's really here with me, but I don't care. Either way, I got to feel like myself again for a night.

We're walking along Main Street, her arm wrapped around me to keep me standing, and a small sense of belonging finally sprouts roots in my heart. I close my eyes and let imaginary Violet lead me home, sure she'll be just another memory when I wake up tomorrow.

five

VIOLET

I BARELY GOT any sleep last night after depositing Noah in his bed. He was asleep the second his head landed on the pillow. I put a glass of water and a garbage can next to his bed to be safe, but planned to check on him today so I wasn't worried. I couldn't stop thinking about him and Gingerbreads all night.

Last night was a shock, but a pleasant shock. I expected seeing him for the first time after years would be horrible, ending with me potentially hitting him. Part of me almost did, not wanting to hear about who he was dating, what he was doing, or his excuses for leaving so suddenly and not returning any of my calls or texts. That maybe yelling at him and storming off would make me feel better, but all those thoughts left my brain when I saw him. Finding out he was in the same spot as me was pretty satisfying, misery does love company after all, and I'm willing to build our relationship up again before we dive into what happened.

One thing I'm seriously mad about was the total lack of information provided by my mother and sister. I need to talk to Mom this morning before all the Thanksgiving festivities start.

Luckily, I've been sitting in the kitchen since seven waiting for her to come down.

After my second cup of coffee she finally emerges, with my dad close behind her. He gives me a kiss on the cheek and heads out to the garage to tinker around with something.

I don't waste any time confronting her. "How come you didn't tell me Noah was home?"

Mom freezes with the pot of coffee in her hands, the 'World's Best Grandma' mug shaking slightly. "What do you mean?" She feigns innocence.

"I asked you about Gingerbreads. You didn't mention him at all," I remind her. "I saw him last night at The Reindeer Hole."

She nods, understanding dawning over her. "Right. Iris and I didn't think you needed to hear about it last night. We wanted to give you a day to be home before bringing your mood down, especially since he just got out of jail. I didn't think you would run into him so soon. I was going to tell you today."

"Wait what? He was in jail?" Confusion washes over me, he never mentioned anything like that last night.

"Oh, sweetie, you missed a lot over the last year," she says, wrapping her arm around me.

"Why didn't you tell me?" I ask.

She sighs. "When he left for college you spent hours crying in my arms before we took you to college. You never got into specifics, but I didn't want to bring up any reminders of him on your first night back. I'm sorry I didn't tell you sooner."

I want to yell at her so badly, but she's looking at me with such caring eyes that I can't blame her for trying to protect me. "It's been years, Mom. I'm fine. Plus we were just friends. He left, and that's the end of it."

"Are you sure it was only a friendship?" she pushes.

"Yes, Mom," I lie, rolling my eyes at her. Now I'm annoyed. If she had told me, I could've been more prepared to see him last night. The fact that he didn't tell me this either is evident that our relationship needs repairing. We never kept anything from each other. Well, I might've kept my feelings about him a secret—or so I thought. It seems like I might've been more obvious about that.

"Whatever you say. I'm sorry I didn't tell you." She kisses the top of my head before letting me go.

"It's okay," I tell her, sipping the last of my coffee. "Did you know Noah came over a lot during high school?" I ask her the question I've been curious about for years before I can chicken out.

Mom laughs. "Yeah, we knew. You two didn't laugh low, and him climbing through your window was never quiet."

"Great, that's not mortifying at all," I whine, my face heating thinking about how I thought I was so sneaky. "Do you have any muffins? I need to run an errand."

Mom tries to hide her smile, pulling a muffin out from the pantry. "Sure do, but be back in time to help cook. Iris is coming over around ten."

"I will, this shouldn't take me long," I tell her, grabbing the muffin and filling a travel mug of coffee. "Love you," I shout, putting on my coat and boots before slipping out the front door. Now it's time to go get some answers from Noah. And maybe find some solutions to fixing both our problems too.

Standing at the foot of Noah's bed I pause before attempting to wake him. He didn't hear me come in, call his name, or enter his room so what's two more minutes of me silently standing here taking in the sight before me.

His head is completely buried under his pillows, and the sheets are all over the place. Almost like he was tossing and turning all night. He's uncovered from the waist up and I realize he must've gotten rid of his clothes sometime during the night. His back is bare as my eyes roam over the muscles all the way down his spine to a pair of dimples I've only seen a few times. I can't tell if he's wearing any underwear, but my desire to find out if he's completely naked consumes me. The image of a naked Noah sends shivers down my spine and between my legs, and I shouldn't be thinking about this while he's lying there.

Taking one last look at the tattooed biceps disappearing under the pillows I lean back and do my best to kick the foot hanging off the bed. I have to hop and almost lose my balance. Thankfully I left the coffee on the kitchen counter.

He doesn't move at all, and I'm not surprised. He really could sleep through anything, even my alarms. One time I tripped over him on my way to the bathroom and he didn't stir. If he didn't wake up on his own, I would have to shake him awake before my parents got up so he could go back to his house before they found him in my room. But I guess it didn't matter since they always knew.

I kick him again with more force and he finally stirs, but doesn't fully wake up.

"Noah, wake up," I hiss, followed by another kick.

"I don't want to go to school today," he groans, burying himself deeper under the pillows. The sheets move further down his hips and my suspicions of a naked Noah are confirmed. I can see the top of his ass and my whole body gets ten degrees warmer. He always slept in his underwear, so I was prepared for boxers—not what looks like the start of a perfectly round ass that I want to bite.

I avert my gaze to the ceiling to avoid staring. "We aren't in high school. Now get up and cover your ass please."

"Wait, what?" I hear shuffling and sheets, but I don't tear my gaze away from the ceiling. "Violet, how did you get in here?" The alarm in his voice is evident, and guilt tightens in my gut for showing up unannounced.

"I borrowed your key last night. I wanted to make sure you woke up in time for Thanksgiving," I tell the ceiling. "I also brought you coffee and a muffin. I would have gotten it from Sips, but they're closed today."

"Of course you did," I hear him say through a laugh. "Can you leave so I can get dressed?"

My eyes betray me, and my head snaps to Noah, who is still lying in bed, now fully covered by his sheets.

"I mean I've seen you without a shirt before—" I start to argue while grabbing a piece of my hair to distract myself. I'm craving to see what his chest is like after all these years. I want to find out if it's as sculpted as his back and if his tattoos are anywhere else besides his arms.

"Violet," he warns.

"Fine, fine. I'll be in the kitchen." I spin, leaving his room and shutting the door behind me.

A few minutes later, he unfortunately appears in dark sweatpants and a hoodie.

"Glad to see our habit of breaking into each other's room is still alive and strong," he quips, grabbing the coffee from the counter and leaning against it.

I spin around on the kitchen stool to face him. "I didn't break in. I simply ensured I would be able to return today. Plus you never broke into my room, I always left the window unlocked for you."

He raises his eyebrow like he might argue with me, but he changes course last minute. There's a tension in the air both of us ignore. "Thank you for checking in on me, but you really didn't have to."

My heart stings at the comment. I don't like him making himself seem unworthy of someone checking in on him. "Did you really think I wouldn't check on you?"

"Honestly?" he starts, pulling the muffin out of the bag and peeling the paper off. "I still wasn't a hundred percent sure you were actually real. I thought it might have been a dream," he confesses.

"It does feel that way, doesn't it? It's weird being here after so long. But we're both here, so..." I shrug, trailing off because I can't figure out what to say without blurting it out. I have so many questions for him, but I don't want to bombard him.

"So..." he says, sipping his coffee.

"I want to help you open Gingerbreads," I quickly say, and Noah chokes on his coffee. It comes out of his mouth and spills down his chest. I hop off the stool and rush over to him, grabbing some paper towels off the counter and patting his chest. It's firm, and I linger too long before he takes the paper towels out of my hand.

"Thanks, Vi. I never did get used to your bluntness."

"One of my many charms," I joke, dropping into a small bow before meeting his eyes. "I'm not joking though. I want to help you."

His eyebrows come together at the center of his forehead, his skin creating a deep groove between them. "Why? How?"

"Why not? I can help with all your business needs, plus baking if you teach me," I shrug.

"Because we haven't spoken in years and you're jumping back into us like we're eighteen again?" he counters.

"Yeah, well, I've got nothing else to do here and you need help. You're really turning down help?" I cross my arms and raise my eyebrow at him.

"This is weird." He gestures between us.

"Why? It's not like we hate each other. Why would anything be weird?" I challenge, knowing full well it's weird. The tension of what happened—or more specifically what didn't happen—hangs between us, but I'm not going to be the first to bring it up. Then there's my feelings for Noah, which haven't gone away, and that was clear when I saw him in bed this morning. Although, that might be my lingering hormones talking and not my brain, since I'm not ready to explore any type of romantic relationship so soon after Greg. I can keep these feelings under control and spend time with my old best friend.

He hums, eyes squinting in contemplation. "It's weird it's not weird," he finally says.

I perk up, pushing off the counter and jumping in front of him. "You mean I can help?"

His hand comes to my shoulder, keeping me still. "Not yet, let me think about it. I'll let you know after Thanksgiving, okay?"

"Fine," I sigh. I suppose I had more time to think about this than he did, so I want to give him time. I head toward the door to give him the time he needs to think it over. "You know where to find me. Tell your mom happy Thanksgiving," I call, closing the apartment door but hopefully not my opportunity to be near Noah again.

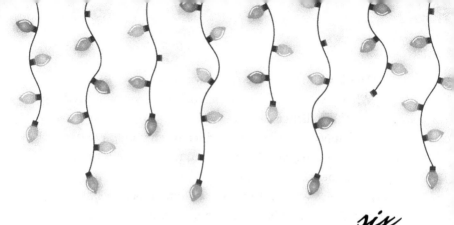

six

NOAH

THE COLD WATER runs through my hair and down my back as I stare down at my erection.

Being hungover always makes me horny. It's usually not a problem since I can wake up and take care of it. But waking up to Violet standing in my room, filling my space with her sweet plum and floral scent, didn't help.

If I had gotten out of bed with her still in the room, she would have seen how painfully hard I was, not to mention other things she probably shouldn't see.

I was able to collect myself enough to join her in the kitchen and listen to her proposal about helping me with the shop.

Now she's gone, but her presence still lingers around me. She's always had that effect on me, and time apart doesn't matter. I always thought I'd be okay if I were to see her again, but all those feelings from high school came flooding back, drowning me. Including the harsh reality of how it ended.

She looked beautiful, standing in my kitchen. Her new red lipstick was something I remembered from last night, and it took all my effort to avoid staring at her lips the entire time she was talking.

I need to get rid of this erection, but I can't stop picturing those damn lips. I need to think about something gross. Like dead bodies. My body instantly cools, so I keep going. Dead bodies at a funeral. Funerals have flowers. A rose is a flower. Roses are red. Violets are blue. Violet has red lips now.

Fuck.

I finally give in to the inevitable, reaching to fist my cock. I don't stop the thoughts of her as my thumb rolls over my tip, spreading the bead of precum around. I groan as desire consumes me. Closing my eyes, I imagine her here with me. Her breasts pressed against me, her lipstick leaving marks on my neck, and her hands bringing me the greatest pleasure I've ever experienced.

The second I picture her getting down to her knees, red lips wrapped around my cock, I spill into my hand, watching it go down the drain. My chest heaves as I catch my breath, but the lack of company leaves me unsatisfied. She's been the center of my fantasies since I was a teenager, but seeing her after so long leaves me the most hollow I've ever been.

I wish I could channel some of her bluntness and tell her how I feel about her, how I've always felt about her. When we were teenagers, I was in no place to give my heart over to someone as good as her. I was starting fights, getting suspended, and driving over to the next town with my friends to ask strangers to buy beer for us. I didn't understand what love should be like, since my parents were the farthest thing from a good example. There was no way teenage Noah would have been able to give Violet what she deserved, even though he tried and failed spectacularly.

Hell, I'm doubtful adult Noah has anything to offer her either. The past eight years have been nothing but moving from job to job since none ever felt right, never at one place long enough to make friends. There was no way anyone, let alone

Violet, would be interested in falling in love with me. I couldn't hold down a relationship for more than a month. Plus was I interested in falling in love? Of course I was, but only with her. It was only ever with her.

There was no hope there, though. Not with how much of a failure I was. It would almost be easier to give in to what people were saying about me. I could start selling weed cookies, buy beer for all the teenagers, or dye all the animals at the rescue. Show this town what they always believed about me was true, that I am worthless and unlovable. But that would be the easy way out.

Drying off, I stare at myself in the mirror, towel hung low on my waist. The one thing on my chest Violet couldn't see staring back at me. It was a good thing I was on my stomach this morning when she came in. If she had seen the tattoo on my chest she would have known what it was and what it meant. I wasn't ready for rejection again.

Thinking about her again, standing in my room, sends shivers down my spine and straight to my groin. I can feel my dick getting harder by the second and don't do anything to stop it. I'm not going to jerk off to the memory of her this time. I could use some pain in my life right now.

Getting dressed, I make sure to put on the sweater my mom got me earlier this month. I told her I would be over to her house soon, but I don't want to get there too early and risk seeing Violet. I need time to think about what she said without her presence actively clouding my mind. Looking around my apartment there are signs of her everywhere. The dried footprints from snow and salt in the hallway, my keys by the door where she left them, the muffin sitting on the counter, and the coffee cup in the sink. I'll have to return that to her eventually. I'm not going to be able to think clearly about what's right for the shop without my feelings for her taking over.

Her proposal isn't a bad idea, but I don't know if I'll be able to work alongside her without asking about how our friendship ended. I need to give her idea more thought, as I remember that my staff is only me, myself, and I, and my heartbeat picks up. I have no idea what I'm doing. I only baked cookies back then, I barely ran the register. Now I'd probably fuck the whole thing up and file the wrong tax form.

When it comes to running a business, I need more help than a few teenagers who are willing to work the front. I need someone who understands how businesses work, or at least someone who can help keep me organized.

With every spiraling thought, I breathe heavier, and my heart pounds in my ears. Going over all the stuff I need to do isn't helping, and I need a day to do nothing. I've been working nonstop since I got home to clean up and fix everything in the shop.

Falling onto the couch, I pick up the video game controller to play a quick game before heading out to my mom's. I put my feet up on the coffee table, where the big box of letters still sits, taunting me. With so many prompts, I'm worried Ginger had too much faith in me, and I won't be able to fulfill each one. Suddenly, I remember seeing one with a prompt that fits the occasion.

Leaning forward I dig through the contents until I find the letter I'm searching for.

Open when you're scared

Kind of ominous, but hopefully it's what I need right now.

Dear Noah,
What the hell are you scared for?

I'll tell you what's scary. Scary is leaving behind everything to someone you believe in, but who might not believe in themself.

I didn't leave you in charge because I didn't have anyone else, I left you in charge because <u>I believe in you.</u> You can call me stupid or insane, but I'm not wrong.

Don't listen to what everyone says about you. You're not some troubled kid who deserves to be unhappy. No one deserves that.

You're kind, thoughtful, and smart—even if you don't see it. I saw it in you the second I met you. Why else do you think I struck a deal with you instead of turning you in? I believed in you.

So take your time to be scared, but then pull yourself together, get off the couch, and start taking action. Life's too short to be scared.

All my love,
Ginger

I can't help but laugh. Leave it to Ginger to write me a letter yelling at me. She's right though, life is too short to be scared. Shutting off my game, I get up to leave for my mom's.

Soon, I'm standing outside my mom's house knocking on the door. Even though I spent most of my teenage years here, it's not my home anymore and I'm uncomfortable walking in unannounced. With my luck I'd walk in on her and her boyfriend in the middle of something I don't need to see.

"Noah, love, you don't have to knock," my mom tells me as she opens the door and pulls me inside. I can instantly smell the turkey already in the oven and I'm already looking forward to my post-meal food coma on the couch.

"Sorry, Ma," I apologize, wrapping her in a one armed hug. I tower over her now, and have ever since my growth spurt at seventeen.

"The turkey is cooking and I could use some help with the sides if you're up for it. Nick is in the living room if you want to say hi." Her eyes twinkle with light and she's almost skipping down the hallway toward the kitchen as she fills me in on the current status of everything.

Guilt settles deep in my gut for being gone for years, especially since Dad died and left her alone. Every time I see her now she's always thrilled to see me, like I might disappear on her again. Ever since moving back to town we've had several long discussions about the past. I opened up to her about how hard it was for me when her and Dad fought. She apologized and told me how much she missed me. It seems like we're finally in a good place.

She's also started dating someone new. Nick has been around for a few years now, and I've met him over the phone once or twice. Coming home to him living here was an adjustment, but he gives me and Mom space when we need it. Plus, he makes her happy, and that's all I want.

"About that. I actually wanted to talk to you about something," I tell her, following her into the kitchen after greeting

Nick with a handshake. I quickly fall into old habits, helping her with whatever she needs to get dinner ready.

"Did you know Violet Emerson is home? You said she wasn't going to be in town for Thanksgiving?" I ask, keeping my hands busy and avoiding looking at her.

She perks up at the question and starts nodding her head like a bobble head. "I did hear on Facebook that she was seen driving through town yesterday. Did you see her?" This is one part of being home I always missed, my mom asking me questions and trying to remain calm when she isn't.

"Yeah," I admit, unwilling to tell her the full truth. "What does she do? Like, for a living?"

"Mildred said she worked in project management. I never understood what that meant. What projects is she managing? Is it a company that only manages projects? Beats me," Mom rambles as she starts peeling potatoes, handing me some to peel as well.

"Nice, nice," I say.

"Why?" Mom asks as we fall into a rhythm.

"I was thinking I could use some help at the shop, business-wise," I tell her.

Her peeler freezes halfway through a slice and her eyebrows shoot up. She's been really helpful about not asking me a ton of questions about what's going on at the shop. "You should ask her," Mom says, hiding her smile behind a bite. "She was always so helpful, she kept me informed about more school activities than you ever did," she teases, elbowing me in the side.

"Yeah, I might," I agree, and we silently return to the potatoes.

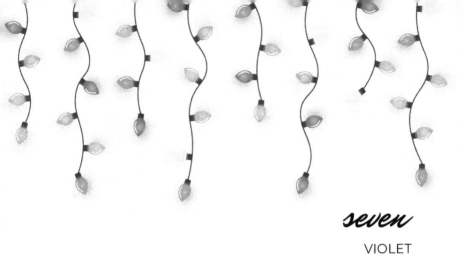

seven

IT'S BEEN a few days since Thanksgiving, and I still haven't heard anything from Noah. I distracted myself by throwing all my energy into Christmas shopping with my mom and building snowmen with Ava. I talked to Iris about the whole situation on Thanksgiving, and she told me to give him time to think it over. Now, my parents are downstairs watching the Sunday eight o'clock news while I take a break upstairs in my room.

Scrolling through my phone, old photos of Noah are the only thing lighting the dark space since I'm too exhausted to turn on the light. Back in high school, we didn't hang out much outside of my room, keeping our friendship mostly between us. There were times when he would check in on me in the halls, but our friend groups didn't overlap. I always wanted to pull him into more activities like the yearbook committee with me, but I was never brave enough to ask.

Most of these pictures are us goofing around in my room. There's the time he let me do his makeup, which I remember was to cover the black eye from a fight at school. Then there's the one where he tried to braid my hair and failed miserably.

He's smiling behind me, while I'm holding out my messy braid and looking annoyed mid eye roll.

A noise outside my window makes me jump and Noah's face pops up a second later. I lock my phone quickly and toss it on the bed, moving to the window to help him.

His palms push the window open, and I'm suddenly a teenager again. Braces crowding my mouth, worrying about what to wear to school the next day, and helping a boy through my window after sunset.

But this time it isn't a boy. It's a man.

He smells much better than he did when we were teenagers, like vanilla. It must be all the baking. He only smelled like stale alcohol the last time I saw him.

He waves me away as he climbs in, determined to do this by himself. I see not much has changed.

"What are you doing?" I whisper-hiss at him, checking behind me to confirm my door is closed. The fear of getting caught by parents sits in the pit of my stomach now that I'm aware they probably heard him climb in. It really shouldn't matter since I'm twenty-six, but I can't help it.

"What? You can break into my apartment, but I can't do this?" he huffs, finally standing in my room. He fills up the space more now, with his taller frame and broader shoulders. A flash of thirteen-year-old Noah crosses my mind, much smaller but as cute as ever.

"We're not teenagers anymore. You could've used the front door," I tell him, crossing my arms.

"But where's the fun in that?" he whispers, shrugging. "I'm glad your dad didn't get rid of the ladder."

"Yeah, funny thing," I bring my voice to a regular volume. "It turns out they knew you were sneaking in the whole time. They probably know you're here now."

"So I don't have to whisper?" he teases.

"No," I tell him. "Now did you think about my offer?"

"Woah, hold on, Vi." He throws his hands up before reaching to take off his shoes and jacket. "Before we get down to business, did I climb through the right window?" He gestures around the room and I picture the last time we were both in here. Everything was different and I thought we were going to be friends forever. The motivational posters that were on the wall from book fairs would have agreed. Then, it all ended in the blink of an eye, and now we're adults and this room is simply here to witness Noah break my heart again, I'm sure. At least this time he's going to let me down in person.

"It's the guest room now," I say, trying not to think about all the time we spent here together.

He hums. "I liked it better when it was your room."

"Yeah," I sigh, moving to sit on the bed. "Me too, but this new mattress is comfortable." I pat the spot next to me and he takes a seat. Memories of him in his bed flash through my mind and I'm glad the lights are still off so he can't see my face flush. But now is not the time to be thinking about naked Noah when nothing can happen between us right now. Especially not when I'm positive he's only here to decline my proposal. If he had wanted me to work with him, he would have been here sooner.

"Not too bad." He bounces on the bed, making me laugh. Which annoys me, because I don't want to get comfortable with him only to say goodbye again. "So are we going to sit here in the dark?"

"Oh, right." I lean over and turn the bedside lamp on, illuminating the room in a dim glow. He's still sitting on the edge of the bed, hands in his lap. "Does this feel weird to you?" I ask him, ready to cut to the chase.

He nods. "I can fix this. May I?" he asks, gesturing to my feet.

"Go for it," I tell him, uncertain what he means but expecting him to break the bad news.

Instead, he doesn't hesitate to stand and grab my ankles. The touch of his fingertips on my skin sends the same electricity through my body like the other night. He turns me on the bed and my heartbeat picks up. I hold my breath watching as he kneels to the floor and my mind runs wild with what he could be doing. Reaching under the bed he pulls out the hidden mattress, and I finally understand where he's going with this.

The second bed is made like the first one, with a thinner comforter. Grabbing one of the pillows from the bed, he hops onto it and lies down. Turning toward me, he props his head on his hand to look at me.

"How's this?" he asks.

I mirror his pose, recreating a position we've been in a thousand times before. My stomach is in knots with the familiarity of having him next to me and I'm starting to wonder why he's dragging this out so much. Maybe he's not going to say no like I assumed. "Much better. Now business?"

"Not yet." He holds up one finger, and my stomach knots further. "Tell me about why you're really in town. I told you my whole thing."

I can't help the laugh that escapes me. "You most definitely did not tell me your whole thing."

"What do you mean?" he asks, furrowing his eyebrows together confused.

"What about the jail thing?" I ask.

Noah lets out the longest groan, running one of his hands over his face. "Fine, you go first and I'll tell you about that."

Satisfied I'll be getting an answer from him, I should probably tell him the whole reason I'm here. Not the abbreviated notes version I would give to anyone else.

"Buckle up because it's a wild ride," I tell him.

He reaches from his shoulder to his opposite waist, making a clicking sound as if he's fastening a seatbelt.

"Last week my company told me I was being let go, effective immediately. Then, when I got home, my boyfriend of three years decided to break up with me and wanted me out of the apartment by Thanksgiving. So when you have no job and nowhere to live, you come home." I get it out all in one breath, thankful to have it all out there.

He stares at me with his mouth open. "Fuck, Vi. That's rough. Are you okay?"

"Yeah. It's probably not a great sign I wasn't heartbroken about it either," I admit. "Now it's your turn." I wave my hand toward him, so he doesn't follow up on that statement. Seeing him again has me starting to realize why I might not have been so heartbroken about it.

He sits up, crossing his legs and leaning his arms against the bed in front of me. Leaning closer, my heart pounds when his face stops inches from mine.

"I killed someone," he whispers.

"You killed someone!?" I shout as his hand flies to cover my mouth. His hand smells like vanilla scented soap, and I want to stick my tongue out and lick him, but I bite my tongue instead. All these old feels are creeping up and taking over my rational thinking.

"Jeez, alert the whole neighborhood, why don't you?" He rolls his eyes. "I'm fucking with you, I didn't kill anyone."

"Fuck you," I mumble behind his hand.

"You wish," he replies, removing his hand from my mouth, but I can still feel the press of his fingertips against my cheek as they heat from the playful teasing I'm used to from him. It's almost like no time has passed between us, but my heart knows that's a lie. "I didn't go to jail. I didn't even get arrested. It's all a big misunderstanding because when I called my mom last month she was in Hanson's and couldn't hear me well. Naturally, she can't keep her voice down so rumors started to spread. Now everyone thinks I was in jail, and there's a different reason each day."

This was part of why I went away for college and haven't moved home yet. Everyone is always in everyone else's business and it's infuriating. I swear everyone already knows about Greg breaking up with me even though none of them know him well, and have only met him in passing once.

"Why did she think you got arrested?" I ask, still needing the truth.

"Let me start at the beginning," he says, clearing his throat and sitting up straighter. "I was at this bar and there was this couple fighting. It was clear the woman didn't want to go home with the guy, but he was drunk and persistent. They were yelling and things escalated quickly when another guy bumped into the boyfriend. He got up and started throwing punches, and I could tell that he was no longer aware of his girlfriend's presence. I stood up and pulled her out of the way right as a stray punch whipped in front of her. She was shaken up and the bartender broke up the fight after calling the police. I didn't want to leave her alone, so I stayed with her until the police showed up. They ended up taking both guys in and wanted to question the girlfriend and me about what happened. The whole time this was happening my mom was trying to call me, but it was too late to call her back by the time I got home. When I finally did call her, she misheard when I told her the other guys got arrested, and thought I got arrested. Then it spiraled from there. That's the big bad story."

"Typical, Noah," I tease, rolling my eyes at him.

"What's that supposed to mean?" he asks, reaching to flick my forehead but I dodge him.

"You're always trying to help out. Every time I saw you at

school you'd help me pick up my books," I laugh at the memory of teenage Noah rushing over to me in the hallway.

"Yeah well, you dropped those books a lot. Someone had to help you." He rolls his eyes, and I keep the fact of how I only dropped my books to see him to myself. "Anyway, now we're all caught up, should we talk about your criminal activity from the other day?"

"Again, I didn't break in," I argue. "But you thought about my offer?"

"I did. I was worried you were only offering because you felt bad for me," he admits. "But now I know you've got nothing to do, I guess I could help you out by letting you work at the shop." He shrugs and crosses his arms. I want to play along with his joke, but I'm too excited.

I lunge forward, throwing my arms around him. "Yay! This will be so much fun."

The movement catches him by surprise and he falls backward, arms uncrossing to catch me. The force sends us sliding back as we hang off the trundle. I'm suddenly aware I'm directly on top of him, his head resting against the floor and my legs still caught on my mattress. His arms are warm around me and there's the slightest squeeze, like he doesn't want to let me go. My thoughts are racing with memories of the dreams I've had about him, but I'm no better than a teenager with raging hormones. The image of his back dimples comes to the forefront of my mind and I would give anything to explore them with my tongue. I want more than anything to rewind time and return to before he left me here alone and heartbroken, but I can't do that.

He holds me there for another moment before pushing us up and righting me on my bed, and I miss the warmth of his hands on me.

"Then we have a deal. Can you start Tuesday morning? I

want to do a few things tomorrow before you start," he says, eyes anywhere but on me.

"Absolutely," I reply, playing with my hair so I don't reach out and pull him to me.

"Perfect." He starts nodding and glancing around the room. "I should go now." He jumps off the bed, quickly putting his shoes and jacket on.

"Right, well I will see you Tuesday," I say.

"Yup. Tuesday." He nods more, opening the window and climbing out. He goes to shut it, and I watch him disappear outside. Before the window fully closes, he's popping his head through the opening, finally looking at me again for more than two seconds. "Two steps forward," he says, pointing at me.

"One step back," I echo, rolling my eyes at the saying he got wrong all those years ago. I've whispered it to myself countless times when I need encouragement. One time Greg overheard me, and corrected me. I attempted to tell him about why I was saying it the wrong way, and he just rolled his eyes. When Noah finally shuts the window, I'm left flustered and excited for what this week might bring.

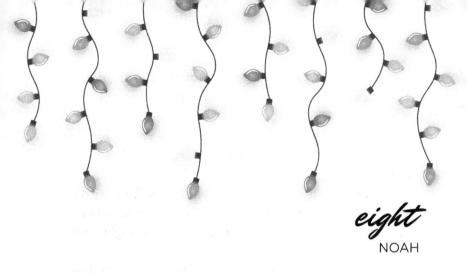

eight

VIOLET WASTES no time arriving at the shop on Tuesday morning, knocking on the front door at 9:00 a.m. I get to the door and unlock it on her second knock. I've been awake for two hours double checking the shop to ensure everything is perfect. Most of my time back in the shop has been spent cleaning, since no one has been here since Ginger died, and there were multiple appliances that needed to be fixed.

"Shit!" Violet yelps when I swing the door open, her glove-covered hand almost hitting me in the face.

I dodge getting punched as I bend and wrap one arm around her waist and spin us inside the shop. The heat of her seeps through her puffy white coat, and my body yells at me. I'm dying to touch more of her. I've been dying to touch every inch of her since I saw her last week. The other night I had to leave her room because I couldn't take it. I wanted to fuse her on top of me and make her scream until she forgot her ex's name. Today she's got her red lipstick on and the desire to push her against the door and see if I can mess it up hasn't gone away. Depositing her on the floor, I quickly shut and lock the door before I act on any of these out of hand thoughts.

"We might need to discuss your customer greeting if that's what you plan on doing. Because I don't think everyone will enjoy it," she quips.

"You enjoyed it?" I smirk, leaning forward and keeping my hands behind my back so I don't reach out and pull her close to me.

Her cheeks flush redder, her nose already red from the cold, and a sense of pride swells in my heart. "That's not what I said." She flicks my forehead like I did to her the other night. "Why did you drag me in here anyway?"

I straighten, putting some distance between us. "I didn't want anyone seeing you come in here. You don't really need to be associated with me." I shrug, walking around her and toward the kitchen. With my luck, Bernice would see her coming in here and call the deputies saying I kidnapped her.

She follows, bumping into the counter with a small "shit" and following me through the kitchen door. "If they got to know the real you, they would love you."

"I highly doubt that," I mumble. She's never been interested in loving me, so why would they? "There's a coat rack back there." I gesture to the door on the far end of the kitchen.

Violet sighs, disappearing through the door only to return a second later sans coat, gloves, and hat. She pulls her long brown hair out of her sweater, letting it drape over the dark green woven material and over her breasts. My mouth goes dry and I avert my gaze away from her chest and back to her face, which is also a bad idea when I land on her moving red lips and realize I've missed whatever she was saying.

"Sorry, what?"

She rolls her eyes. "I was saying you need to make more of an effort around town."

"Who says I don't make an effort?" I bite back.

She crosses her arms and tilts her head at me, her annoyed expression only making me smile.

"Fine. Explain." I lean against one of the counters.

"You need to show them you're not scary. That you *smile* and have *fun*," she explains. "Get your Christmas spirit showing."

"That sounds awful." I wrinkle my nose at the idea of mingling with the town. The Christmas stuff I'm fine with, but the idea of talking to a bunch of people who hate me? Not as appealing.

"I'll help you, we can go together." She gestures between us. Everyone always loved her when we were in high school. It's part of the reason I stayed away from her in public; I didn't want her to get tainted by my bad reputation. Even now, I don't want that, but I need help if I'm going to get anyone to come to this shop.

"And if I say no?" I ask.

"I'll leave," she counters. And damn it, she knows my weakness.

"Fine." I fold immediately, hesitant to lose her again for another second. "But I need to show you around here first."

"That works. Plus what I have in mind isn't open yet," she grins at me.

"What is it?"

"Ice skating, Christmas Festival, maybe a sleigh ride too!" She gets louder with each item until she's yelling. "I missed Christmas last year because my ex wanted us to spend it with his family. I'd love to do everything this year, which works out for you," she explains.

I've done my best to actively avoid all things town related since being home, but they seem less daunting if she is going to be there with me. Ever since the Christmas tree incident I avoided all things Christmas Festival. The look on my face must give away my feelings because she keeps going before I can continue.

"Listen, it sounds horrible, but you can't reopen this shop and expect everyone to flock in here." She gestures around the room. "They all think you were in jail, and you know how they are. They won't believe us if we tell them you weren't actually in jail unless we show them you're good first. And that you won't ruin anything."

The use of "us" and "we" in that sentence spreads warmth through my chest, but I can't show her that yet. "You mean I can't bake cookies in silence and live a life of solitude on Main Street?" I tease instead.

"Noah. . ." Her annoyed expression returns.

"Violet. . ." I retort. Her eyebrows raise and I can tell she's one teasing comment away from yelling at me. She always liked putting me in my place, and I always enjoyed being yelled at by her more than I was willing to admit. "Fine," I relent.

"You also need to decorate your windows." She points toward the front of the store where the windows are still covered in newspaper.

"Do I have to?" I sigh. Every year there's a window decorating contest for all of December. All the local businesses on Main Street participate and a winner is crowned on the last day of the festival.

"Your windows are currently covered in newspapers. Yes, you have to," she tells me sternly.

"I don't have any decorations," I tell her.

She huffs. "Have you looked around? I'm sure Ginger has some somewhere."

"Fine, you're right. I'll do whatever you say without complaining, but I make no promises for any faces I make. And I'll look for the decorations."

"Perfect." She nods her head once in satisfaction. "Now give me the tour."

I walk her through everything in the kitchen starting on the farside. She nods along as I explain how the large mixer works, which reminds me that I need to look into ordering a second one. I point out which ovens are the trickiest of the four and tell her the top one can't be on if the flash freezer is on or it will trip the breaker—another thing I haven't gotten around to fixing yet. The middle of the kitchen is equipped with large stainless steel tables with various supplies underneath them while the back has a large sink for dishes.

Leading her to the pantry in the corner I tell her about all the ingredients and why they're organized the way they are when I realize she isn't paying attention. Instead, her back is to me and she's staring into the empty kitchen. I wonder if she's having trouble being here without Ginger. When I first got here, I sat on the counter not moving for several days—letting the memories of Ginger take over until I was comfortable enough to invade her space without it feeling like an intrusion. Her presence hasn't left though, and I'm ninety percent sure she might be haunting the shop. I can still see her running around putting together a last minute order that she blamed Bernice for not getting it in time, but we all knew Ginger forgot about it.

"Vi," I say to get her attention, reaching and placing my finger and thumb on her jaw to turn her head my way. "You need to pay attention. Did you need a notepad?" I ask. She was always better at studying than I was, and her notes always shocked me with how thorough they were.

Her eyes widen, and it takes all of my strength not to guide her to my mouth. We stay frozen for what I'm sure is an eternity before she breaks the silence with a whispered, "Sorry, no. I can remember everything. It's weird being here without her."

"Don't apologize. I had a hard time with it too," I tell her.

"It's a lot to take in," she admits. "I don't really bake, so this is all new to me."

"What was your previous job?" I ask, knowing the answer but hesitant to leave this small space yet and attempting to redirect her focus on something else.

"I did project management. So the farthest thing from baking," she lets out a small laugh.

"True. We can go slow," I tell her. "Plus I haven't even shown you the mess of the office. That's where you'll be most helpful. I'm a lost cause when it comes to that stuff. Want to check that out and bake your first batch tomorrow?" I don't want to overwhelm her with baking, and the paperwork might be easier for her today. All of this stuff came back to me easily once I got started, but I know it won't be the same for her.

"Yeah, that will help," she agrees, following me out of the pantry and toward the office.

"Also for tomorrow, make sure you don't wear a sweater, it's going to get hot in here," I tell her, spinning around and leaning against the door frame. Her cheeks flush and I realize what I said. "You know, from the ovens," I clarify.

"Right, right." She nods. "Good tip."

"Anyway, here's the office," I say, moving out of the way and letting her into the madness. The space is tiny with several filing cabinets and one desk stacked with piles of paper.

She walks in, and the lightbulb that needs changing soon illuminates her in a maddeningly soft way that has my hands itching to grab ahold of her and never let her leave my side. Maybe after she helps me open the store, she'll leave instead of torturing me with her presence.

"Is any of this organized?" she asks wearily, slowly spinning toward me with her eyebrows high and eyes wide.

"Not really, but when was Ginger ever organized?" I laugh

because if I don't I might cry at all the work she left behind for me to figure out.

"Well, guess it's time to get to work," she says, rolling up her sleeves and I see two small butterfly tattoos on her wrist that I want to touch.

By lunch time, I decide to call it a day because we're both already exhausted trying to decode Ginger's messy handwriting and filing system. She agrees and bundles up, moving around like she still isn't comfortable in the space. Then she's out the door and I'm left standing alone in the kitchen with her floral scent lingering in the air.

nine

VIOLET

LAST NIGHT I BARELY SLEPT. I kept replaying the moment in the pantry with Noah.

One moment my mind was running through everything he told me, trying to remember how all the appliances worked and shake off the feeling of Ginger lingering. The next my skin was on fire from his touch as his gaze locked with mine. I thought he might pull me into a kiss, but he didn't. Part of me was disappointed. But he had plenty of moments to kiss me before, and never did. I'm not sure why he would now. I wish I was brave enough to give in to my feelings and be the one to kiss him, but I keep worrying that he's going to disappear again after I just got him back.

Today, I'm standing across from him with a metal table between us and bowls, measuring cups, and cookie cutters scattered around. We accidentally matched both in black T-shirts and blue jeans, and it's taking everything in me not to crack a joke about it. He's wearing his shirt better than me, though. His tattoos are fully visible and it's hard not to stare at them, I'm dying to find out the story behind each one. I want to ask if he's noticed the small tattoos on my arms, and if they're affecting him the same way his are driving me crazy. I avert my gaze and sip my coffee, grateful for the caffeine to help wake me up.

"You have to finish and toss that before we start," Noah says, pointing at my coffee. "I don't need you spilling coffee into the cookies."

"What?" I gasp. "I would never spill, how could you say that?" I throw my hands in the air, the coffee spilling out of the top and burning my hand. He raises one eyebrow at me. "Okay, fair. Did you finish yours?" I ask, licking the coffee off my hand.

He taps his empty cup on the counter. "I did. Thank you for getting me some. You didn't have to stop at Sips."

"Of course, and yes I did," I say. "Also, Sydney says hi. I didn't realize she was home too."

He nods. "She's probably one of the only people in town who likes me."

"Have you been hanging out with her a lot?" I ask, killing time as I finish my coffee. Noah and Sydney were always friends. She was always nice to me, and I wondered if she knew I had a secret crush on him. I was always jealous of how much time she spent with him.

"Not really. I've been busy here," he says.

I nod through the last sip of my coffee, tossing it into the trash can once I'm done.

"Okay, Coach," I say, pulling my hair into a ponytail. "Put me in, I'm ready to bake some cookies."

"Go wash your hands," he rolls his eyes at me.

"Aye, aye, Captain," I salute him and wash my hands in the sink. The soap smells like vanilla and I'm starting to wonder if he favors vanilla-scented products.

Returning to the table I see all the supplies he has set up. The circular cookie cutters are larger than I thought they would be. Picking one up, I inspect it.

"These are pretty big," I say.

"Yeah, well, remember how you could never finish one?" he teases. I would go to Gingerbreads sometimes when he was working just to see him somewhere that wasn't school or my room. The cookies always left me full by the time I got halfway through one, but he always helped me finish them later that night when he would come to my room.

"I bet I could fit my arm in these." Then, without thinking, I stick my arm through the cookie cutter and slide it up my arm.

"Violet," he shouts. "They're sharp." He barely gets it out before I nick my bicep with the metal.

"Ouch, shit." I jump, pulling the cookie cutter off my arm as a small red line appears in its wake right above the tattoo that's there.

He groans and rolls his eyes as he comes around the table and grabs my hand, pulling me to the bathroom. "I told you it was sharp," he chastises.

"Yeah, well curiosity killed the cat I guess," I say back, inspecting my arm when we stop in front of the sink, squeezing so more blood comes out of the cut. It doesn't hurt much, which makes me want to squeeze more. Whenever I get bruises I have a bad habit of repeatedly poking them. It drove Greg crazy, which made me want to do it more.

He shakes his head at me as he grabs a small first aid kit from below the sink, used to me constantly hurting myself with small bumps and bruises. He opens a small Band-Aid package and pours some hydrogen peroxide on a paper towel before taking my arm into his hand.

His grasp isn't hard or harsh, not as tight as my own. His fingers aren't cold but warm on my skin that's still chilly from the cold winter air. I'm frozen as I watch him clean the cut and put the Band-Aid on. His fingers linger on raised lines in my skin.

"Pretty tattoo," he says softly, pushing on the Band-Aid one last time to secure it in place.

"Thanks, it's a violet and an iris, for obvious reasons," I tell him, thinking of how Iris has a matching one on her arm. "Sorry about getting blood on your cookie cutter," I apologize as he leaves the bathroom to toss the cookie cutter in the sink, giving it a quick rinse first.

"You didn't grow out of that?" Noah crosses his arms and leans against the sink, facing me and I resume my spot next to the center table.

"What do you mean?" I ask.

He points at me with his pinky. "The accident proneness. You've got a cut on your finger too."

I glance at my hand, the Band-Aid from when I arrived is gone now and the cut is healing. "Cardboard cut," I explain with a shrug.

"Ouch, those are the worst," he winces.

"Yeah, well, when you're trying to get out of your place in a hurry you don't really care about bumps or bruises," I say quickly, remembering flashes of me shoving all my belongings into a box and not bothering to pack them neatly or label the box. "Anyway, what are we baking today?"

He doesn't question the subject change, and pushes off the sink. "First, we need to put on gloves. Especially since you have a cut on your finger," he says, pushing a box of gloves down the table to me. "No one is going to eat what we bake today, but you'll need to get used to wearing them. For cookies, I was thinking we'd start small and easy. How do snickerdoodles sound?" he asks, walking into the pantry and turning around as his full frame fills the doorway, his arms stretched above him holding the frame. The position causes his shirt to rise, showing a small sliver of skin and I avert my gaze quickly when I notice a trail of hair disappearing into his jeans. My body heats thinking of where it leads.

"Those are my favorite," I admit, picking up a mixing cup to distract myself from ogling him.

He smacks the frame, making me jump. "That's it then," he exclaims. "They're one of my favorite Ginger recipes. We'll do a small batch."

He reaches to one of the pantry shelves and grabs a small wooden box before returning to the table. Moving around the table to get a better look I see it's filled with hundreds of index cards I assume were once white, but are now tinted yellow with tears and stains all over them. He flips through the cards until he finds the right one, pulling it out with a satisfied "ah-ha!" which makes me laugh. I follow him around as he heads back toward the pantry, pulling different containers off the shelf and handing them to me. I try to recall which ones are which from yesterday but being in here only reminds me of Noah's touch on my face. My cheeks flush and I look to the ceiling, urging them to return to a normal color before he turns around.

I follow him out to the table, and he takes the containers from my arms and sets them on the table, along with the ones in his arms.

Turning to me, he sports the cheesiest grin I've ever seen on him. "You want to know the secret ingredient?" He leans in and whispers, and I can smell his vanilla scent.

"Love?" I tease.

"No, focus," he whisper-yells, picking up one of the small containers. "Cream of tartar. It's what helps them stay soft and chewy."

I wrinkle my nose in disgust. "Tartar? Isn't that raw meat?"

"For fuck's sake, this is going to be a disaster," he grumbles under his breath and drops his head.

"It is not." I smack his arm.

"Sorry, sorry," he laughs, throwing his hands up in surrender. "I didn't realize you knew literally nothing about baking. I'm going to have to teach you more than I thought. Tartare is raw meat, but take off the e and you have cream of tartar. It's a dry, powder-like, acidic byproduct of winemaking. Tartaric acid is one of the main ingredients, hence the tartar," he explains, pointing the container at me. My confused gaze meets his. "You didn't understand any of that? Did you?"

"Nope," I pop the p. "Not a word."

"Well, it's different," he says.

"Perfect," I nod. "Tell me what we need and how much." I rub my hands together, picking up a glass measuring cup.

"First, glass is for liquids." He steals the cup from my hands. "Use these for dry ingredients," he says, handing me a red plastic measuring cup.

I note the difference in my head, not sure why it matters, but I trust he knows what he's talking about. He slides the index card between us, pointing out all the different measurements and I try to keep up, but they all blend together. I keep glancing at it to confirm the tablespoons didn't morph into teaspoons.

I gather the right amount of flour as he pulls out a small Kitchen Aid mixer from beneath the table, plugging it in.

"Probably should test this to make sure it didn't break overnight," I barely hear him mumble as two things happen at once. One, Noah starts the mixer. Two, I dump the flour into the bowl of the mixer.

A puff of white powder blinds me as I hear him swear and turn the mixer off.

Embarrassment washes over me and I hope I suddenly activated latent powers of invisibility so I can sneak out of here and move to a remote cabin in the mountains where I don't have to interact with anyone.

"Open your eyes," I hear him chuckle through his words.

Light slowly creeps into my eyes as I open them. Noah is covering his mouth, trying not to laugh at me. Taking a deep breath I glance down at myself to see my black T-shirt is now white, and I can only assume so is my face. Reaching to wipe my cheek, my hand gets covered in flour.

"You missed some," he says while biting his lip, pointing to the other side of my face.

"This isn't funny," I whine, trying to act annoyed about it but his laughter is contagious.

"This is one hundred percent funny," he teases. "You're not a super talented baking assistant." He tosses a dish towel my way.

Wiping my face off I can tell there is flour in places where flour shouldn't be, like my ears.

"Maybe you hand me stuff, and I'll do the mixing," he suggests.

"No, I can help mix." I slam my hand on the table, landing right on an egg and crushing it.

"Yeah, not happening," he says. "Go over there." He points from me to the other side of the table, far away from the mixer. "Measure out the other ingredients."

"Fine." I cross my arms, stomping over to where he told me. "I guess that's fair."

I manage to avoid any more mistakes as Noah prepares the dough. He explains everything as he does it, and I grow more confident in asking clarifying questions. By the end, he lets me help put the cinnamon and sugar mixture over the cookies before baking them. They only need about ten minutes in the oven and the bakery already smells amazing.

He's cleaning the table as I get the remaining flour out of my hair.

"You wanted to go ice skating today, right?" he asks when I

return. He's taken the cookies out of the oven, but I keep myself from diving in and burning the roof of my mouth.

"Yeah, does that still work for you?" I ask, positioning myself next to the cookies.

"Sure thing, but you might want to go home and shower first," he suggests, glancing me up and down.

My cheeks heat, again, and it's like any look this man gives me has my knees wanting to give out. "Very true. I'll do that and come back here. But do I get to taste one of these first?" My fingers tap along the table toward the cookies.

"Of course, they're all for you," he says, pulling a to-go box out from below the table. "Bring them home, and tell your mom I say hi."

ten

NOAH

VIOLET KNOCKS on the door of the bakery right as the lights on Main Street brighten the street. Sending her home to clean up made the afternoon go by as slow as possible. Every time I heard something outside, I checked the window to see if she was back.

Opening the door, the street lights illuminate her fuzzy hat and coat. Her cheeks and nose are flushed from the cold like this morning, and she's holding the container I sent her away with. Doubt creeps in that her family didn't want to eat the cookies, or worse, they hated them, and now she's here to quit, never to be seen again.

"My mom sent me back with leftover lasagna," Violet says, interrupting my spiral and stepping inside.

"So she liked the cookies?" I ask, closing the door behind her and putting my coat on.

"Obviously, Noah." She rolls her eyes like this fact was somehow supposed to be obvious to me. "They were delicious, and we ate all of them already. Kind of ruined dinner, which is why we had so much left over. Here." She holds the container out toward me.

"Glad to hear it," I casually say, but I'm internally doing cartwheels. "I'll trade you. Lasagna for keys." I pull a ring of two keys out of my pocket, handing them over and taking the food from her.

"Keys for what?" she asks, her eyebrows wrinkling in the cutest way I've ever seen.

"The shop. That way you don't have to break in anymore," I tease. "You might not be used to keys, but we're adults now. There's one for the front, one for the back."

"For the last time, I didn't break in." She hits my arm while simultaneously putting the keys in her pocket. "Ready to go?"

"Yeah, just let me put this away. And please tell your mom thank you for me," I say, disappearing into the kitchen. I'm still in shock that her family thought of me.

Ten minutes later we're lacing our skates on a bench outside the rink. It snowed earlier, so there's a fresh layer coating almost every surface. The Christmas lights strung all over town reflect in the snow to create a glittering effect.

The rink is mostly full of families and couples, and I feel out of place. I can sense all of their eyes on me as they skate by. Looks of confusion and disgust mark their faces as they try to hide their scowls—they're probably all expecting me to ruin Christmas somehow. I want to go home and lose myself in a video game or a TV show.

I hear a groan to my left, and all those feelings dissipate when I see Violet's face bunched in a frustrated frown.

"You okay over there?" I ask, finishing my last knot.

"I can't get this damn skate on," she huffs.

I shake my head and let out a small laugh at her frustration. Carefully moving to the ground, I kneel in front of her. "It's all about getting the right angle so your foot slides right into the skate," I repeat what my mom told me when she first taught me to skate. Grabbing the skate in one hand and her foot in the other, I guide her foot into place.

"Why is it so stiff?" she asks as I move on to the next foot, wiggling the skate around in the air.

"Rentals always are. Wait," I pause. "Have you *never* been skating?"

"Not really?" she says it more like a question, like I should remember if she's ever been before.

A million images of her getting hurt run through my head. Falling and cracking her head open. Breaking her arm. Twisting her ankle. Her hand getting run over by a skate. Run over by a reindeer? More like run over by a twelve-year-old.

"What do you mean not really?" I ask, putting air quotes over 'not really.'

"I was always too scared about falling," she admits. "I would watch Mom and Iris from the edge, and my dad would get me a hot chocolate and sit with me. So I've been here before, but never on the ice. It'll be okay. You know how to skate, right?"

I shake my head quickly. "Not really, I only went a few times as a kid. Why did you think this was a good idea if we can't skate?"

"Because it's what people do." She's got both hands on my shoulders now, and she leans in closer to me. "We can do this, I believe in us."

"That makes one of us," I mumble, averting my gaze from hers before I lean up and kiss her. After tying her skates, I help her up, and we do an awkward skate waddle over to the rink's entrance. We're about to step onto the ice when someone calls Violet's name.

I recognize the shrill voice from various not so subtle insults throughout high school and don't have to see her to confirm the identity of the woman with poorly dyed blonde hair now standing in front of us.

"Violet Emerson, I thought that was you! How are you?" she shrieks far too loudly.

"Brittany, hi. I'm good, how are you doing?" Violet politely returns the generic greeting.

"Fabulous, as always." Brittany flips her hair, split ends flying behind her. "I heard you weren't going to be in town this year. You were supposed to be with your boyfriend, right? Everything okay there?" She leans closer to Violet, lowering her voice with a pitying tone I want to comment on, but I don't want to embarrass Violet. Brittany hasn't even looked my way, and I wonder if it's because the last time she saw me I was crashing her graduation party.

"Everything's fine," Violet lies through a smile and cheery tone, wobbling on her skates. I reach out to keep her upright and her shoulders relax. "Thanks for the concern though. I'm here with Noah, actually."

Brittany finally registers my presence and gives me a disapproving look before fixing her face into a fake smile. "Nice to see you, Noah," she says with a click of her tongue before turning to Violet. I nod her way but I'm less focused on her, trying instead to figure out if Violet was implying we are here together or here as friends. I zone out for the rest of their conversation as they talk about the Christmas Festival and try not to overthink it when Violet leans further into me.

They finally end their conversation and Brittany leaves without saying goodbye to me. Violet lets out the biggest sigh I've heard from her in a while.

"You okay?" I ask, moving to face her.

"Fine," she says, pursing her lips. "I always hated her. She was a nightmare to plan the dances with. She only came over here to get gossip out of me. But don't let her ruin our night, let's skate," she says with a nod of her head and heads toward the entrance.

"Do you need one of the pushers?" I point to a small child on the ice holding onto a metal pusher to keep them upright, hoping she says yes because I want one.

"No, I Googled it. Push and glide, right?" she shrugs, stepping out onto the ice and gripping the edge of the rink.

I guess if she's committed to doing this, I have to be committed to doing this too. I'm not going to let her go out there alone. And I'm sure as hell not going to be left behind.

Stepping out onto the ice I push off the wall and let myself glide. I'm too nervous to move my feet and I slowly come to a stop a few feet to Violet's side, who has moved down the wall and away from the entrance.

"Are you going to let go of the wall?" I nod her way.

"Are you going to stand up straight?" She sticks her tongue out at me, mocking my hunched over position. My arms are stretched out in front of me to help keep me balanced, and if I stand upright there's a fifty percent chance I fall over. But I'm not going to let her tease me.

Slowly, I lower my arms and straighten my spine. Violet lets go of the wall and starts to slow clap, but the movement causes her to fall onto the ice. My instincts kick in and I try to reach out and catch her. Instead I join her on the ice as a group of kids skate by laughing at us.

She's laughing though, and I drown out the world around us and focus on her laugh. Her smile is so wide it reaches the corner of her eyes, and I can't help but laugh along with her.

After some more stumbling, and crawling, we're both standing and holding onto the wall.

"Maybe if we hold hands it will help balance us?" she suggests, moving away from the wall and reaching her gloved hand out toward me.

"Or we'll both fall, no matter what," I sigh, reaching out and grabbing her hand anyway. Her hand in mine feels so right, like it's the thing I've been missing for the last eight years. "Let's stay close to the wall, and you move to the inside." I pull her toward me, switching our positions on the ice and trying not to get lost in her floral scent as she passes in front of me. With her near the wall if a twelve-year-old crashes into us it will be me who gets hit instead of her.

"Okay, so on three, push and glide," she says, nodding her head like she's building up the courage. "Like two steps forward."

"Okay, one..." I start.

"Two..." Violet chimes.

"Three." I push off with one of my skates and she lets go of the wall. We glide forward less than a foot, both of our arms sticking out on either side, until we come to a stop.

"We did it," she cheers, looking over at me. I can see the Christmas lights twinkling in her blue eyes, and I want nothing more than to make her happy, so I push off again, but harder.

This time we go a bit further, and the next time Violet joins in. Before I know it we finish one lap around the rink without falling. It might've taken us half an hour, but we didn't fall.

She also never dropped my hand, something I noticed about halfway through. I don't want her to drop it now, so I say, "Another lap? Maybe a bit faster this time?"

"We can do that," she nods.

An hour later, we've done three more laps, and our hands are still fused together. There were a few times we almost went down when she grabbed my arm for balance, but I managed to keep us upright.

I keep telling myself there's no way she could be interested in me, and I'd have no shot with a girl like her. That the way she's holding onto me so tight is only because she doesn't want to fall. But when we finally step off the ice and she doesn't drop my hand, I can't help but forget about all my worries and wonder about if she thinks we could be more than friends.

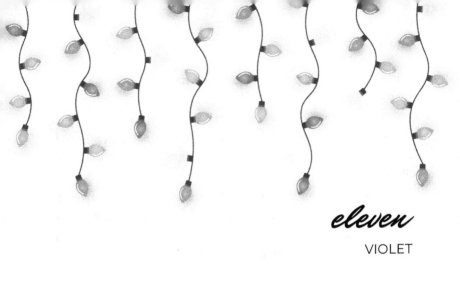

eleven

VIOLET

"WHAT DO you think of starting with five flavors?" Noah asks me the next day.

I'm having a hard time focusing on the task at hand when all I can think about is ice skating last night and getting him close to me again. I almost spill flour all over myself again so I can take my shirt off to see what he would do. I can't help but want to walk the line of friendship between us and stick one toe over to test him. See how much I would have to push him before he gave in, if he wants to give in at all.

"Five is good, not too many and not too little. What about this one?" I pick up one of the recipe cards from the table. They're all scattered out in front of us, including several different versions of a chocolate chip cookie. Noah dumped them out when I arrived this morning with coffee and a muffin, telling me he wasn't set on which cookies to bake for reopening.

"That's more of a fall flavor," he says, plucking the pumpkin pie cookie recipe from my hand. "I want to stay on theme with Christmas flavors like peppermint."

"But don't you plan to open after the new year?" I ask,

confused as to why he would want flavors that are out of season.

"Yeah, but you know how much this town loves all things Christmas," he says. "I bet I could do Christmas all year, and no one would complain. Maybe that's how I get them to like me."

I think about high school and what Ginger would do around the holidays. I remember a cookie with marshmallows on it that melted on my tongue. Or I'm making that up, and Noah snuck them on the cookie for me. Either way, I remember it being around Christmas.

"Is there a hot chocolate one?" I ask, searching for it.

"Maybe?" he says. "I've gone through these so many times now, and they all blend together. There should be a gingersnap one in here somewhere too."

"Shut up, that would be so cute," I shriek, causing him to jump.

"Jeez Vi, I don't think everyone in Sips heard you," he says, covering his ears.

"Come on, gingersnaps? Gingerbreads? Ginger!" I throw my hands in the air.

"I know." He rolls his eyes, stepping closer to me and pulling my hands down, pinning them to my side. "Why do you think we need to find it?"

He's so close to me now that I smell the lingering scent of coffee on his breath. I'm becoming more aware of his fingers around my wrists with each passing second, and how if I stick my tongue out it wouldn't take much to reach him. But I shouldn't do that. Why am I thinking about licking him right this second? Oh god, I've been silent too long.

Violet, say something.

"At least buy me dinner before you pin my arms."

Violet, no. Not that.

"I'd make you dinner *and* dessert," he's quick to quip, keeping his hands around my wrists.

Don't say it.

"I thought I'd be the dessert," I smirk at him, and his grip tighten around my wrists before he lets go and backs up. I hear him mumble something, but I can't make it out.

"You're going to be such a distraction, aren't you?" he asks, returning to the index cards.

"Maybe, but I'll also be helpful." I pause, picking up the recipe we've been searching for and hoping I sound normal. Meanwhile, my heart is pounding like I recently ran a 5K and my whole body feels like it's on fire while I overthink my dessert joke. But if Noah had hated it he would have said something instead of his small jab about me being a distraction. Focusing back on the card in my hand, I hope my face isn't giving away my racing thoughts. "For example, here's the gingersnap one."

His eyes light up when I pass it over to him, and I notice they're lighter today. The green is even brighter than when I first saw him, but it must be the lights in here.

Returning my focus to our current task, I find three more of the recipes we need while he locates the last one. I'm going to need to focus on cookies and not Noah if I want to get through this day without any accidents.

"Okay so we've got the gingersnap, hot chocolate, peppermint, and candy cane brownie. Plus chocolate chip because you need at least one classic," he says, switching between the cards as he lists them off. I fought for the double chocolate chip one, but he said that would be too much.

"Perfect, the chocolate chip will be great for kids who aren't ready to step out of their comfort zone yet," I say, stopping myself from pointing out the double chocolate one would have done the same thing.

We quickly fall into baking, me refraining from disaster and

Noah directing me. I manage to keep myself from yelling "yes, Chef" every time he asks for something. I guess he's a baker and not a chef, but I'm also doubtful he would care. I also know if I said it I wouldn't be able to stop myself from giggling.

He teaches me as he goes, explaining the perfect way to whip the chocolate mousse for the hot chocolate cookie. Each cookie has its own special topping or secret ingredient to it that makes it unique, and the kitchen has started to smell so good that my mouth is watering. It doesn't help my concentration that every time Noah mixes the batter or picks up anything heavier than a teaspoon, his forearms flex and reveal the perfect combination of tattoos and veins.

Working with him is helping me forget about my train-wreck of a situation. Greg hasn't crossed my mind in a few days, and the more time I spend with Noah the more I wonder if I ever loved Greg. Maybe he was convenient for where I was in life. I never had as much fun with him in the past several years compared to these last few days with Noah. My heart never skipped a beat with Greg the way it does with Noah. Whatever is happening between us is more real than anything I ever had with Greg, and I'm starting to wonder if he can sense it too. I had the same feeling years ago, though, and he left. Which makes me think I'm making up what might between us.

"What do you think about going to the tree lighting tomorrow night?" I ask, crushing the last bit of the peppermint pieces.

He sighs before answering, and I see his shoulders drop. "Do we really have to go to the festival?"

"We talked about this," I remind him. "You have to show your face around town. They have to see you engaging with town activities so they stop making up rumors about you. Is there something else that makes you not want to go?" I pry when he avoids eye contact with me like he did any time he had something he didn't want to tell me.

"Ugh." He runs his hands over his face. "This is embarrassing to admit, but I applied with the committee for a stand at the festival, and they denied me."

"Oh, I'm sorry." My heart sinks for him. I want this town to understand he's not a bad guy. I don't understand why they can't find it in their hearts to give him a chance.

"Don't be, it's not your fault. They really don't like me. They really can't get over the Christmas tree incident." He shrugs defeated. "But I'll go, just be aware I won't like it."

"Then think of it like you're going with me because I want to go," I tell him, trying to cheer up the conversation. "I haven't been in a few years and the tree lighting was always one of my favorite parts of the festival. Plus my family will be there, so you'll have plenty of buffer if anyone tries to start anything or kick you out."

"Will Iris fight Bernice for me?" he teases. He's probably remembering the same memory of Iris picking me up from school once and yelling at someone who was making fun of my dress. She's always quick to defend the people she likes, and I've had to stop her countless times from yelling at Bernice and the other town gossips when they're being dramatic.

"You know she would," I reassure him, knowing she cares about him because I do.

twelve

NOAH

MY MOOD SEEMS to be cheerier than normal as the lights on Main Street turn on. It might have to do with the fact I've seen Violet every day for the past week, and now I'm headed to see her again. Even though I saw her a few hours ago, there's a skip in my step as I head to the festival. I told her I would meet her there, since it didn't make sense for her to backtrack to the shop.

My stomach's in knots, and it gets worse the closer I get. I can't tell if I'm nervous about being at a town event, or if I'm excited to see Violet again. She brings back so many feelings from high school that have me feeling young and invincible again. So invincible that I could take on the town gossips. I don't care if they boycott me. I'll bake cookies for me and Violet, and feed them to her like grapes, unless she doesn't actually want that from me.

I'm starting to realize I've never wanted anything more than her, and I don't care what happened eight years ago. Ginger would probably hit me over the head for saying that. I'm sure she's got a letter titled *"Don't be an idiot"* somewhere in the box that I haven't found yet.

I hear Violet before I see her, her warm laugh echoing over the chatter of everyone else. Weaving around several groups my eyes finally find her. Her white coat is as big as ever, with her matching hat and gloves to go with it. She's adorable and I want nothing more than to scoop her up and kiss her.

Her family surrounds her, and I forgot how much Iris and Violet look alike. Iris has aged well, and if I didn't know they were seven years apart I would've guessed they were twins. My mom told me Iris's husband is nice, and I can tell she's right by the way he gazes at Iris. He's holding who I assume is their daughter in his arms since she's clearly a mini version of Iris with her matching hair and eyes; even her nose is the same. Violet's parents' backs are to me, and my stomach twists more. Ever since she told me they knew I used to sneak into her room I've dreaded seeing them again.

She spots me before I can spiral too far, her red lips growing wider as her hand waves wildly in the air.

I'm returning her wave when her parents turn around. I thought I'd be met with glares, but they both seem happy to see me.

"Everyone remembers Noah, right?" she asks her family, reaching out and pulling me to her side when I get close enough.

"Nice to see everyone again," I say, focusing on not tripping over my feet from the force of her pull. My stomach has only gotten worse, and having her invade my space isn't helping. But no part of me wants her further away from me, so I squeeze her hand in mine.

"Hey man, I'm Jacob. And this is Ava," Iris's husband speaks up, reaching out his free hand to shake mine, introducing me to the two people in this group I've never met.

"He doesn't look dangerous," Ava chimes in and I see her mom's eyes go wide as my cheeks heat.

"Ava, do you want to go meet Santa?" Jacob is quick to distract her, and I'm grateful for it.

"Santa!" Ava shouts, wriggling out of her dad's arms and running off into the crowd. He shoots me an apologetic glance before running after her.

"Let's go too. It was nice to see you again, Noah," Violet's mom says, pushing her husband toward the direction Ava and Jacob fled, Iris close behind them.

"Sorry about that," Violet apologizes for Ava once we're alone.

"It's fine, at least she didn't hear a worse rumor." I shrug.

"Do you want to go get hot chocolate?" She points behind her toward the food stands. "Maybe browse and shop? We have about an hour until the lighting."

"Lead the way." I step to the side, dropping her hand and gesturing for her to go ahead of me.

Instead, she grabs my hand and pulls me into the crowd and my heart grows three times bigger. Weaving around families and couples she makes a beeline for the hot chocolate stand. It reminds me of the way she hurried from class to class in school. She prided herself on never being late, thanks to her fast pace and weaving skills. Then, there was me, who waited until there was one minute left to get to class to actually start moving. I thought I was being cool, but I was being stupid. Being late got me my fair share of detentions.

She orders two hot chocolates with extra marshmallows, and I have to drop her hand to reach for my wallet. The second I'm done paying and my wallet is secured she takes my hand in hers and I have to stop myself from smiling like a giddy teenager.

"It's so cold out, these should help warm me up," she says, squeezing my hand. I don't question why she's so cold when her gloves are fuzzy and look plenty warm, because I don't want to risk her dropping my hand.

Collecting our drinks the smell of cocoa instantly fills the air. I can't remember the last time I had hot chocolate. Violet's blowing on hers with those mesmerizing red lips, that bright coloring having become one of my favorite new things about her. I don't know when she decided to start wearing it all the time, but I'm not complaining.

We walk around with our drinks, and luckily she doesn't burn herself or spill it. She points out all her favorite stands, talking about how she could buy more presents for everyone. She's so animated when she talks about her family, and I wonder why she never moved home.

It's not long before her family joins us again. Ava is also carrying a cup of hot chocolate and a stuffed reindeer with her name on the collar. I assumed when they returned Violet would distance herself from me. Instead, she pulls me closer to her and hangs onto my arm. Her nose and cheeks are almost as red as her lipstick, so I pull her under my arm and rub her arm to warm her up. She rests her head on my shoulder and I try to refrain from cheering.

"Mom, when does the tree turn on? I'm tired," Ava groans through a sip of her hot chocolate.

"Should be soon, why don't we go over and get a good spot?" Iris tells her.

The tree is large, but not Rockefeller Center large. The local tree farm, Winter Farms, donates one every year. It's decorated to the max with garland and ornaments. I can see the unlit lights strung around the branches going all the way to the star on top.

"So we wait until they plug it in?" I whisper into Violet's ear, not wanting Ava to hear me.

"I mean, yes, but once they're on, the Christmas season has

officially started," she whispers back, putting a finger over her red lips to tell me to shut up.

Before I can reply, the head of the committee, Holly, is stepping on a platform with a microphone. She runs the Chamber of Commerce and is in charge of the festival this year, though I have a feeling she isn't the one who denied my application for a stand. With the three town gossips all on the committee I bet Holly didn't see the application before they tossed it in the trash.

She takes her time thanking everyone for being there and how community and forgiveness are everything this time of year. A sentiment that makes me roll my eyes because it seems like forgiveness is the one thing I'll never get from this town.

The crowd, including Violet and her family, countdown with Holly from ten until the tree lights up. The white lights brighten the space around us, and people gasp like they've never seen lights on a tree before.

"Kind of anti-climatic isn't it?" I whisper, aware it's going to piss her off.

Right on cue, she elbows my side. "Shut up, it's beautiful. All the lights sparkling and lighting up the festival? It's perfectly Christmas," she tells me.

She's staring at the massive tree, eyes glowing with pure wonder. But I'm staring at her, those blue eyes sparkling with the reflection of the lights. "You're right," I say. "It's beautiful."

thirteen

VIOLET

"CHANGE OF PLANS," I say in lieu of a greeting when Noah opens the door the next morning.

"I get to stay home?" he groans, pulling the toothbrush out of his mouth. I try to avoid staring at the tight T-shirt and how it hugs his arms and chest in the perfect way.

He wasn't very happy with me when I told him we were going to the festival again today. The tree lighting last night was a good start, but one trip to the festival isn't going to change the town's mind about him.

"Nope. We have to take Ava to see Santa," I inform him.

"What?" He glares at me, the divot between his eyebrows as deep as ever.

"Hi," Ava jumps out from where she was hiding behind me.

"Holy shit," he practically screeches, jumping back several feet.

"Auntie, he said a bad word." Ava latches onto my arm, pointing to Noah.

"Noah didn't mean it. Did he?"

"I mean what do you expect when—" I glare at him and widen my eyes before he sighs. "No, I didn't."

"Perfect, now finish getting ready and let's go." I wave my hand at him.

"Didn't she see Santa yesterday?" he questions with a raise of his eyebrow.

"I need to go every day or he might forget who I am," Ava explains. "There are a lot of kids in the world. Plus, I remembered something else I want."

"Where's your mom?" He squats so he's eye level with her.

"Checking peoples eyes so they finally realize they need glasses," she quips.

He only laughs at her bluntness, standing and heading into his apartment to get ready.

I bend and fix Ava's jacket, which has become unzipped since sitting still isn't in her vocabulary. "You were in the other room when your mom said that."

Ava shrugs. "I have good ears."

"I guess so." I shake my head at her, noting I should watch what I say around her.

The walk to the festival is filled with Ava asking Noah questions about himself like I'm not even there. She runs through all of the favorites first, with some answers surprising me, like how his favorite animal is a red panda. After she's satisfied with his answers she moves on to asking what he does. He tells her all about the shop, and he promises her one free cookie a month, and two on her birthday.

The festival isn't as full during the day as it was last night, but there are more kids running around today. The smell of peppermint and chocolate are in the air and it's perfectly Christmas.

"Lovebug, do you want to sit on Noah's shoulders?" I ask, stopping us at a nearby bench.

"What? Isn't she too big for that?" He groans looking at Ava, who is smiling ear to ear.

"I am not! My daddy does it all the time." She crosses her arms, hopping up on the bench.

"She's light, you'll be fine," I tell him. "The town seeing you with a kid will automatically get you points. I don't know why I didn't think of it before." Having him hold onto Ava will also keep my hands off him.

I wonder if he noticed how I kept grabbing his hand last night, like he was my own personal magnet. But he didn't pull away once, comfort flowing easily between us. It wasn't strange to fall into those familiar touches again. It was almost like we never lost touch.

I'm starting to realize whenever I would hang out with him in high school we would always find ways to touch each other. It was always friendly touches and teasing hits, never leading to anything more. The more comfortable we got with each other, the more frequent those touches got. Like when we would watch movies or TV shows on my laptop. Our legs were always touching in at least one spot while the laptop rested on his lap and my head on his shoulder as we squeezed together on the twin bed.

I've been so lost in the memory of him I missed Noah putting Ava on his shoulders. His hat is now askew as my niece adjusts herself. His eyes scream "get me out of here" and I can't help the laugh that escapes from my lips.

"What?" He groans, securing her legs by placing his arm over his chest.

"Your hat is crooked. Let me fix it," I say, stepping closer and adjusting it so it sits evenly across his forehead, his green eyes shining bright from the reflection of the snow.

"I can see so much more from up here," Ava cheers, bouncing and causing him to sigh while making sure she doesn't fall off. "You're taller than my daddy."

"Can you see Santa from here?" I ask her.

"Almost." She squints, like it will help her find him. "Let's go!"

"Yes, ma'am," he huffs, rolling his eyes and heading off in the direction she points him.

It doesn't take us long to find Santa, and along the way Ava keeps talking about how she feels like a giant. Noah finally seems all warmed up to her, and I realize my idea of putting her on his shoulders was a bad idea. Seeing him effortlessly banter with her is starting to give me baby fever when we're not even together.

With Greg, I never imagined him as a dad. There were a few times I pictured what our kids would look like, but I was never excited about it. That probably should have been a red flag, but I ignored it like all the other ones. Meanwhile, Noah is easy to see as a dad. I thought seeing him bake was hot, but seeing him interact with Ava is much hotter. But then again, everything he does is hot.

Noah plucks Ava off his shoulders once it's our turn. Santa instantly remembers who she is, greeting her by name, and her eyes light up. She spends a few minutes telling him more things she wants. Noah steps closer to me while we wait by the side, grabbing my hand and sending shivers down my spine. I try not to react, instead focusing on what Ava is listing off. Maybe I could get her one of those things since I still need a gift for her.

When Ava hops off Santa's lap and comes skipping over, Noah drops my hand. I sigh at the loss of his touch, even if it was through our gloves. The brief moment of disappointment is replaced by happiness when Ava steps between us, grabbing both of our hands to walk through the festival.

She leads us to her parents' stand with the Emerson's Eyes blue and white logo large above their heads. Iris is in the middle of an eye exam with an older man, while Jacob is at the front and waves at us. Ava is quick to drop our hands and run around to hug her dad. He props her up on the edge of the table in their stand, her legs swinging over the edge, and pours her a hot chocolate from the small drink dispenser they are using so people have a warm drink after their eye exam. Noah doesn't waste time taking my hand in his as we approach and I might need to talk to my sister about this as soon as I can.

"Thanks so much for taking her to see Santa again," Jacob says once we're close enough.

"Of course, how are the eye exams going?" I ask, nodding toward Iris.

"Pretty good, we've already gotten two new patients. Probably three after she finishes here." He pauses, directing his attention to Noah. "Do you need a free eye exam? You get a free hot chocolate," he says, tapping the top of the drink dispenser.

"Oh, I don't know. I can see pretty well," he stumbles through the sentence like he wasn't ready to speak.

"Come on, give Iris something to do." I nudge his shoulder.

"Fine," he grumbles, stepping around the side and into the stand as Iris finishes and sends the older man to Jacob.

"Are you braving the exam?" Iris smiles when she sees him coming her way.

"Looks like I am." He glares at me as Iris takes him to her exam area.

Once Jacob has the older man scheduled for a full appointment he wastes no time leaning toward me, whispering, "What's going on there?"

"What do you mean?" I lean in and whisper.

"With N-o-a-h," Jacob spells out Noah's name, but I'm pretty sure Ava can spell and is already acting like she isn't listening to us.

"Nothing, I'm helping him with his shop and gaining favor with the town," I tell him. Jacob didn't meet Iris until after I had left Evergreen Lake, so he never got the chance to see Noah and I together.

"Seems like something is going on." His eyebrows wrinkle together right under his hat. "He looks at you the way I've been told I look at Iris."

"Like what?" I ask, aware of exactly what he's going to say because I've been the one to call him out before.

"Like you're his whole world." Jacob isn't whispering anymore as my cheeks flush.

fourteen

NOAH

AFTER DAYS of teaching Violet how to bake, she suggested winding down tonight with pizza and a Christmas movie. Not wanting her to leave, I was all too quick to agree. Spending so much time with her is bringing me right back to when we were in high school. Every time I make her laugh I'm ready to throw my doubts out the window and ask her for a second chance. She hasn't stopped wearing the red lipstick, and my dreams have been filled with nothing but her. One dream was just her slowly putting lipstick on and it was torture, and I don't know how much longer I'll be able to last.

Now we're on my couch as *Home Alone* plays, the pizza long gone. We would watch this one to start every Christmas season, with her cuddled next to me. The volume would always be turned low since we didn't want her parents to come find us, useless in retrospect. We're mirroring that same position now, she's curled next to me but we're under separate blankets. If we were under one I would pull her closer until she was sitting on my lap. My dick seems to like the idea and I have to take a deep breath to calm down. I also keep my arm around the back of the couch and away from her shoulders so I'm not touching her too much.

In addition to being surrounded by her presence, I'm starting to realize how having her here makes me want to do better. I don't think eighteen-year-old Noah ever realized how much confidence she had in me. I always assumed she had the underlying thoughts everyone else wasn't afraid to say. How I was worthless and I wouldn't amount to anything. But maybe she always saw me for who I am and not some fuck up. Maybe I could shake off the pressure of trying to prove myself and learn to be happy with where I am right now. Especially since I had the one person I've wanted for years next to me.

"You know I thought about you a lot in New York," I tell her when she nuzzles closer into my side. I figure if she doesn't want to hear it we can let the movie play. But I can't let another moment go by without clueing her into the fact I might want more from her.

She perks up at this, lifting her head and looking over at me. "Do tell."

"Well, passing by any flower shop automatically brought you to mind. One time I bought a bouquet of just violets. My roommate was confused when I came home with flowers for myself."

She doesn't say anything, but she won't stop staring at me.

"What?" I ask, laughing nervously, worried this might have been a bad idea.

"That's really sweet," she says, and I think she might be about to cry. I don't want her to cry right now, so I think of something else to tell her. "I also thought of you every time I saw a rat."

"Noah!" she yells, hitting me right in the chest. "That's so mean." She laughs, wiping her eyes and I relax.

"Because you hate them, that's all," I defend myself. "New York has a lot of rats."

"Ugh, I do hate them. Their tails freak me out." She shudders. "Things reminded me of you too. Especially whenever I saw a fallen Christmas tree."

"Touché," I say, tipping an imaginary hat toward her. I want to ask her to elaborate on what actually made her think of me instead of her joke, but I don't want to push her if she isn't at the same spot as me.

She smiles at me, grabbing my arm off of the couch and pulling it around herself as she rests her head on my shoulder. I don't move as she gets comfortable next to me. I don't want to mess this up, going eight years without her tucked next to me was a mistake. Even if she didn't want anything back then, it seems like we've moved past that and fallen into our familiar ways.

Her fingers play with mine and they move to touch the small tattoo on my wrist. I have no doubt she can tell my pulse quickens as I watch her trace the lines with her fingertip. It's my oldest tattoo, faded in looks but not in memory. I'll never forget the night I got that one.

It was one of the nights Violet could hear my parents fighting from her open window. I had wasted no time climbing down my roof and into her window to escape like every other time before. She never questioned me either, I think she could tell when I didn't want to talk about it. I'd climb in and she would already have the trundle bed pulled out, and I'd collapse onto it and join her in whatever she was doing. Half the time it was homework, so I would just lie there and listen to her write. Her pen would always find its way to something else though, whether it be my skin or my shoes. She was always doodling something somewhere. My Converse high tops were fully decorated with her drawings because she was too scared to draw on her own shoes, afraid her parents would yell at her. I didn't mind being the canvas for her.

One night when I came over she was experimenting with stick-and-poke tattoos, adding a violet above her knee while wearing these tiny pink pajama shorts that drove me wild. I watched her finish it and asked for one next. Right on my wrist next to a scar I had gotten from walking through one of my parents fights and getting hit by a piece of a plate as it broke against the wall.

She asked me what I wanted and I pointed to the one she had done, telling her, "I like that flower. How about that?"

She nodded, and got to work after that. Both of us stayed silent as she gave me a matching tattoo. I thought she might tell me to do something different. But I wanted part of her with me anywhere I went.

It was the first time she had her fingers on my skin that long, and I never wanted her to stop touching me. No one's touch ever lingered on my skin like hers did. Having her touch the spot again is different from all the other times she's touched me since being home. There's something more intimate in the way she slowly runs the same path over the lines sending shivers down my spine. I've fully forgotten about the movie now, only able to focus on her and how her breathing has become heavier.

"You still have this?" she finally asks, gaze never leaving the tattoo.

"Of course," I say, lifting my other hand under her chin and tilting her head to meet my gaze. "I couldn't cover up my first."

"Why not? It's only a silly little flower," she says through a jagged breath and I can see the rise and fall of her chest quicken as I hold her face in my hand.

I pull her closer with the slightest tug under her chin, and she follows shifting to fully face me, dropping my wrist. Her floral smell fills the space between us as my now free hand moves to the base of her neck and over the goosebumps on her skin. "It wasn't just a flower," I whisper.

Her eyes close and her mouth parts as I run my thumb along her neck to her pulse point. The beat of it quickens and my dick hardens under my sweats. I realize this is the closest we've ever been with this kind of quiet tension. The heat of her breath on my lips and the last bit of my self control is disappearing.

"Hey, Vi?" I whisper again.

"Yeah?" Her response is breathy as she keeps her eyes closed.

"I'm going to kiss you now, okay?" I say before I can back out of the one thing I've dreamed of for years.

"Okay," she replies, sucking in a breath.

fifteen

NOAH

MY LIPS ARE on hers in a second and it's like my whole world is changing in slow motion.

This kiss isn't fast and passionate like I thought our first kiss would be, but slow and sensual. I want to take my time with her, cupping her jaw with both of my hands and keeping her fused to me. The tips of my fingers find their home in her hair as I devour her soft lips.

Running my tongue over her lip, I can't help but need to taste more of her. I don't know if she's going to give me more than this, and I want to taste every part of her while I have the chance. She opens to me without any question, and the second our tongues touch she lets out a moan that travels through my body straight to my dick.

She pushes into the kiss to get closer to me without taking her lips off mine. With the push of her tongue against mine, I move my hands down her body and to her hips until soft skin above her leggings greets me. Gripping her hips, I lift her onto my lap.

Our lips part when she lets out a small yelp, letting me

guide her to where I need as both of our blankets fall to the side. Her hands fall to my shoulders as her knees bracket my legs but she doesn't sit fully. Instead, she hovers above me, staring at me as I stop myself from burying my face between her now eye-level breasts that are moving with the fast pace of her heavy breathing. I'm not sure if this is really happening right now, but I don't want it to stop.

She's got the same shocked expression that I'm sure is on my face. But the second our eyes lock all the shock fades away as her blue eyes light up and her lips break out in a grin that wrinkles the corner of her eyes.

"You have no idea how long I've dreamt of doing this," I admit through a disbelieving laugh as I guide her to sit fully on my lap, dropping my head and letting a groan out as she settles over my dick. The friction of her weight and all our clothes is just what I need at this moment.

"Me too," she says before grabbing my face in her hands and pulling me to her. This time the kiss is less reserved as she slips her tongue into my mouth and nips at my lips.

I guide her hips to move over me and she listens, rocking against my erection. When she moans into my mouth my balls tighten and I encourage her to move faster. I haven't touched myself to the thought of her since the morning in the shower, which might have been a bad decision since I don't know how much longer I can last with her like this.

"Violet," I gasp between kisses. She slows her movements but not her mouth as she moves to kiss along my jaw.

"Yeah?" she asks, and I can feel her smile against my skin. Her fingers scrape along the back of my neck, sending a full body shiver down my spine as I try not to thrust between her legs.

"If we keep going I'm going to come in my pants," I admit to her, and I'm not embarrassed at how close she has me. She could stand there and I would be three seconds away from losing it.

"Okay," she says through another grin and nip at my jaw, sprinkling kisses along my cheek and back to my mouth as she picks up her pace.

"Okay? Not okay, I want you to come with me," I tell her. We've waited so long to have each other and if this is the only time I get to kiss her I want to leave both of us satisfied.

"Too bad," she giggles, and I want to be mad about it but her giggle has so much power over me that I would do anything she wanted. She bites my lip before sucking it into her mouth, and I realize I'm still guiding her hips over me.

I finally give into the inevitable conclusion, shifting her on my lap to get her right where I need. She moans and I capture it with my mouth, tasting every inch of her mouth and letting her sounds fill my veins. She moves over me and I'm suddenly in high school again, about to come in my pants on a couch with a hot girl on top of me.

With every rock against my dick I'm closer to the edge, unable to focus on kissing her and letting the feeling of her here with me take over and overwhelm me. Violet holds my head in place with her nails in my hair and her forehead against mine. My moans and her panting fill the space between where our mouths hang open.

Everything is so right and so real, but the second she gasps my name I lose it. The orgasm is anything but calm as it crashes into me, sending me spilling into my pants. It's one of the best orgasms I've ever had.

After what seems like years, I open my eyes to see her smug face grinning at me, no doubt proud she was able to unravel me at her touch without taking off any of my clothes.

"Wait, what about you?" I ask through my heavy breathing, running my hands from her hips to her knees.

"Give me one second," she says, grinning at me with a twinkle of mischief in her eyes.

I'm frozen in a post orgasm haze watching as she reaches into her leggings. I can't see what she's doing, but her hand moves quickly rubbing against me through our clothes as she gets herself off on my lap. She drops her head back, and I tighten my grip on her knees to keep her in place above me. Her breasts heave and her neck is so bare that I want to leave my mark there later. It's not long until her legs start shaking and she's screaming as her orgasm hits her.

I burn this image of her mouth open, cheeks flushed, taking her pleasure on my lap with me at her mercy. If I died tonight, I would have no regrets.

"Fucking beautiful," I decide to not keep my thoughts to myself as she looks at me, smile wide and lipstick smeared. I hope it's covering me.

"You too," she giggles, leaning forward to kiss me one more time before hopping off my lap. "I should probably walk home though. I told my mom I would be back tonight and I don't want her waiting for me."

"You're not walking home alone," I tell her. "I'll go with you." Her house is only a few minutes from here, but it's late out now and the movie credits are the only sound filling the apartment.

"No way, then you'll have to come back alone," she lets a yawn slip past her lips while shaking her head.

"You're not walking if I'm not going with you," I say firmly.

"Fine," she huffs, standing and leaving the room.

"Where are you going?" I call after her.

"To bed, I'm tired. I'll text my mom," she calls from the direction of my bedroom.

She might be trying to kill me, because when I enter my bedroom she's already located one of my shirts and she's pulling it over her head. Her legs are bare and I see the pile of her clothes discarded on the floor. All I can do is watch her as she moves around my room like she lives here as she climbs into my bed. I'm embarrassed I didn't make the bed and there are dirty clothes scattered all over the room.

"You can't be serious," I groan.

"It's not a big deal. We used to sleep next to each other all the time," she says, adjusting the sheets and fluffing one of the pillows.

"Those were separate beds," I remind her. I don't know how well sleeping next to her after what we just did will go. It's going to take everything in me to stop myself from pulling her against me and fucking her all night until she needs help standing. But as much as I need to get lost in her body, I don't want us to move too fast and screw this thing up now that we've crossed the friendship line.

"Sorry, do you want me to move to the couch?" Her face flushes and she stops all movement.

"No, I can take the couch. I need to clean up first though," I laugh, gesturing to my crotch where there is clearly a mark from our activities.

"Right, sorry. But really I can sleep on the couch," she stutters, dropping the pillow and moving to leave the room.

"Vi," I say, grabbing her arm as she passes me. She stops, staring at me and I desperately want to know what's running through her mind. "You don't have to be sorry about anything," I reassure her. "I have no regrets about tonight. Only that we should have done it sooner."

That gets a laugh out of her as the worry leaves her face and her eyebrows become unpinched.

"I'm fine sharing the bed if you are, we're adults, right?" I suggest, hoping to ease her into my bed even if it means I might not get any sleep.

"Okay, but I have to pee first," she nods, leaving the room and heading to the bathroom. I watch her turn the light on and spin to face me. "I don't have any regrets either," she tells me before shutting the door and I realize I'm in for a long night.

sixteen

VIOLET

THE SMELL of coffee wakes me up the next morning, instead of the smell of Noah curled next to me. Part of me wanted to wake up tangled in each other and hear him tell me how he needed me. We'd get lost in each other and he would slip into me with whispers of how right we felt together. We'd give into our long building urges and explore each other. Memories of last night on the couch flooded my dreams, but Noah seems unaffected. Instead he stayed on his side of the bed and woke up before me. Yet ever since Jacob pointed out how Noah looks at me I haven't been able to unsee it.

Every moment with him had started to turn into this bomb I'm tiptoeing around, afraid to set it off because of how he didn't want to continue anything with me—not even our friendship—eight years ago. But last night, sitting next to him and watching a movie felt too good. It was too familiar, too easy, and I didn't care anymore that he left me without a word. I wanted to live in the moment. Then, when he admitted he thought of me, I wanted to cheer and tell him there wasn't a week that went by without me thinking of him too.

When he kissed me there was no way I was leaving the

couch without making him fall apart for me. I'd waited too long to see it. But now I'm trying to stop thinking about his moans and gasps to cool my libido down before getting up.

Looking around his room I can't stop thinking about how easy it would be to fall into a life here with Noah. He's barely moved in and I could help him get truly settled. I could help him run the shop and be close to my family again, and find a place where I belonged. Maybe staying could be my Christmas present for my mom. She'd never ask that of me, but I know she'd love for me to live closer. It would be a better gift than the scarf I bought her.

I get dressed in my clothes from yesterday and head out to the kitchen, where Noah is pouring two cups of coffee. His shirt is tight around his chest and arms, paired with a different pair of dark gray sweatpants from last night and messy hair that I want to make messier. I could get used to the sight of this.

"Morning, Vi," he says in a hoarse voice, handing me a cup.

I thank him, bringing the coffee to my lips and letting the liquid warm me up.

"Do you want breakfast?" he asks me.

"No, I'm going to swing home and change then I'll come back. You wanted to focus on Ginger's office today, right?" I ask him, trying to remember the schedule he laid out but all I can think of is how I can get him to touch me again.

"If you don't mind. I have an appointment at nine, so how about ten? I really am a lost cause when it comes to running a business." He sighs, and I realize he's probably embarrassed by his lack of knowledge. He hates not being good at things, but lucky for him this is what my business degree was built for.

"Sounds like a plan." I finish my coffee and head out, stopping myself from going over to him and kissing him goodbye like I want to. If I got close to him right now I'd end up dragging him into the bedroom and I don't know if we're there yet. I want to ask him what last night meant to him, but I can't take a rejection right now.

My parents are already at work when I get home, so I take my time to shower and change. I'm about to leave with a bagel and a travel cup of coffee when my phone dings.

MOM

FYI I had Dad put your boxes from high school in your car. I figured you could take them to Noah's and use his dumpster to get rid of things you don't want. Have a good day! Xoxo Mom

I laugh and roll my eyes at her signature texting end. I've told her on several occasions she doesn't need to sign off on every text, but it doesn't stop her.

VIOLET

Thanks Mom. I'll be home later tonight, don't wait for me. Love you!

MOM

Love you too! Xoxo Mom

Turning around, I grab my keys and wallet since it sounds like I'll be driving to the shop instead of walking. I assumed there wouldn't be too much to go through, but when I climb into the front seat and I can't see out the rear or the passenger seat window I realize Mom might have had a good idea about taking all this to Noah's. It's not like I need any of this stuff anyway.

Parking outside of Gingerbreads, the key Noah gave me lets me enter through the front and bring the boxes in. It seems all too familiar, like this is something I could do everyday, and it's starting to scare me how easy it is.

I can hear him grumbling in the office as I move my way through the kitchen.

"Are you doing okay?" I ask, leaning against the doorframe of the small office.

"I'd be better if Ginger organized anything in here," he groans, gesturing to the mess of papers surrounding him on the floor. When he finally looks at me, I'm grateful I'm leaning against something because I might have fallen over from seeing him.

"You got glasses?" I ask, pointing to my face. Hoping that sounded cool, because inside I'm screaming. Iris really did me a favor, and I'm going to have to thank her later. The wide round pair frames his face perfectly, and the tortoise pattern balances his green eyes and dark hair. He looks delicious and I want to push him to the ground and have my way with him. But that's not what I'm here for.

"Iris said I needed them, and I shouldn't drive without them," he tells me. "She had this leftover pair from someone who never picked them up with the same prescription. What do you think?" he asks, moving his head around to show me every angle.

"They look good. They suit you well," I say, trying to force the heat creeping into my cheeks to stop.

"This might take us longer than I anticipated." He redirects the conversation to the papers on the floor. "I want to have everything organized so when someone inevitably calls the IRS on me, I know where to find stuff."

"No one is going to call the IRS on you. Plus I love to organize," I tell him, squatting to meet his eyes. "It's going to be okay, you've got me now."

His eyes twinkle and before he can reply a knock from the front door echoes through the shop.

"Are you expecting someone?" I ask him as he stares toward the front, eyes wide.

"No," he answers. Followed by a whispered, "Go answer it."

"No," I say. "It's your shop, you go answer it."

He groans, standing up off the floor and heading out of the office. "So much for *'you've got me now,'*" he mumbles as he passes me.

I follow behind him, stepping behind the front door so whoever it is can't see me. He rolls his eyes and takes a deep breath before unlocking the door.

"Hi, Noah. I'm Bernice." Her high voice fills the small front end of the shop, and I see him wince.

"Hi Bernice, we've met. A few times actually." He reaches out and shakes her outstretched hand.

"Right, well, can never be too careful. Anyway, I wanted to come by and apologize for rejecting your festival stand submission," Bernice says, and my heartbeat picks up.

If she says anything rude to him, I'm fully prepared to kick her ass.

When he doesn't reply she continues, "I thought it over and a Gingerbreads stand would be the perfect addition to the festival," she pauses. "To honor Ginger of course."

"Of course," he agrees. "Thank you, Bernice. I really appreciate the reconsideration."

"Well you know me, always sticking up for the little guy," Bernice chimes and I have to cover my mouth before a laugh escapes. "You'll be stand one thirteen and you can start on Friday."

He takes a piece of paper from her, a map of the festival with one thirteen circled.

"One other thing," Bernice starts as he stares at the map in shock. "The Emerson girl is working with you, correct?"

"She is," he answers, quickly glancing in my direction.

"She mentioned you might be interested in supplying the sugar cookies for the sugar cookie decorating contest," Bernice continues.

"Oh did she?" He reaches behind the door and tries to swat at me, but I jump before he can reach me.

"Yes, would that be true?" Bernice asks.

"I'd love to do that, if you don't mind," he tells her.

"Perfect. We usually do two hundred. Thank you for donating those. I will see you on Friday," she tells him, and he flinches when she says 'donating.'

"See you then, thank you again," he replies, shutting the door and locking it again. He slowly spins toward me and I can't read his face. "You're dead, Vi," he says through a laugh, pointing at me with the map in his hand.

When he steps toward me I make a beeline for the kitchen, and he isn't far behind me.

"What did you do?" He tries to sound stern but I can hear the laughter in his voice.

I run around the table in the center and stop when he's across from me. I'm already panting, I don't think I've run this fast in a while. "Don't kill me," I beg. "I talked to her at the festival before you got there."

"So dead," he says, shaking his head and running around to the side of the table.

"Noah, no!" I yell, trying to run around to the other side, but he's too fast. My view turns upside down as he spins me around and over his shoulder. "Put me down!" I yell, hitting him in the ass.

"I'm going to throw you in the snow," he tells me as he carries me through the kitchen and outside the back door.

"Don't you dare, I was helping you," I protest, as the December air causes goosebumps to break out all over my skin.

"Yeah, well, I've already committed to this," he says, lightly dropping me into a snow pile.

Luckily, the snow is fluffy, but I scream when the cold goes up my shirt. He looks guilty and stretches his hand out to help me up. Instead of standing, I yank and pull him toward me. He clearly isn't ready for it, and easily collapses into the snow next to me.

"You're welcome, you asshole," I say through a laugh.

"For what?" he groans, wiping snow off his face. "For going behind my back? For pulling me to the ground? For risking my new glasses?"

"Listen, I was helping you. She likes me, and she wasn't supposed to mention me," I tell him, sitting up on my elbows.

He falls deeper into the snow. "That doesn't make it any better. But thank you," he says to the sky.

"Of course. You deserve to be there, and we'll show them why," I say confidently, standing and reaching my hand out to him.

He takes it, and doesn't pull me down with him. "Guess we need to go to the basement and find Ginger's festival stuff," he says, brushing the snow off his clothes and heading into the shop.

"And maybe we could find the window decorations, too," I suggest, which receives a grunt from him.

Suddenly, he stops in the doorway, causing me to bump into him. "Wait, also why would you suggest donating cookies? That's so many to give away for free." He turns toward me, crossing his arms.

I roll my eyes, stepping around him and into the warmth of the shop. "We'll be fine, it'll be great points with the town. Trust me, two steps forward..." I start.

"One step back," he groans, but with a smile on his face.

seventeen

VIOLET

I HAD every intention of talking to Noah about what our mutual orgasms meant for us moving forward, but there hasn't been time. After Bernice gave us the approval for the stand we've spent the last three days running around like chickens with our heads cut off. From digging around the basement for supplies and getting cookies baked so we don't sell out, there hasn't been a moment where we aren't moving.

I wanted to bundle the cookies in Christmas themed bags with ribbons, but since we had no time to order them we had to improvise with cardboard boxes Ginger had left over. Noah got lucky and found a small display warmer to keep some of the cookies warm. Some are meant to be served cold, so that was good for us. But there's something about warm chocolate chip cookies that hits differently, so we both agreed the warmer was a necessity.

He finally got it to work this afternoon, having to run to the store a few times to get different replacement parts. It seems like Ginger never liked to buy anything new, something he has complained about a few times.

We're bringing the five holiday flavors he's been teaching

me to bake and selling them at a discount as a special festival price. I was able to borrow craft supplies from Iris—well Ava—to make pricing signs and labels for which cookies we had available.

"What do you think of this?" I ask, leaning on the stool to look at the sign on the table as Noah pulls the last batch of chocolate chip cookies from the oven. I ended up commandeering half of the table to get these done tonight. The red and green paint is perfect for Christmas.

He transfers the cookies to a cooling rack and comes around to where I am, pulling a stool next to me and taking a seat. "They look great, Vi," he says, picking up one of the signs and admiring it. "You've always been good at anything artistic."

"Thanks, I'm really happy with how they turned out," I say.

There's a moment of silence before he whispers, "I'm really nervous about tomorrow."

I turn toward him, taking his hands into mine, forcing him to face me. I rub my thumbs along his skin and say, "It's going to be okay, I'll be there with you. You've got to take those steps forward to get anywhere."

"I know," he says, finally looking at me. "I just have a bad feeling about it."

"That's understandable. How can I help you?" I ask, uncertain what would be best for him right now.

"I need a distraction, you said you brought boxes over right?" He stands, heading to the front of the shop instead of waiting for my confirmation.

"I did, old stuff from high school," I tell him, following him through the kitchen door.

"Let's do that then, I don't want to think about cookies anymore," he says, effortlessly picking up a stack of three boxes at once, something that shouldn't be as hot as it is.

I manage one box, figuring four should be enough to

distract us for now, and follow him into the kitchen. He sets the boxes on the floor and drags one of the large trash cans over between the stools. Setting my box on the table, I pick up the art supplies to create space for us to go through everything without ruining the signs I made.

Noah plops onto his stool, and he looks exhausted when he runs his hands over his eyes and down his face as he tries to stifle a yawn.

"We can call it a night," I tell him, the last half coming out through a yawn.

"No, no. Let's get at least one of these done. If we go to bed now I won't be able to stop thinking about tomorrow," he says, and I don't miss his casual use of 'we.'

Sitting on my stool, I open the box on the table to see it's filled with nothing but papers. We both grab a handful, spreading them out in front of us. It seems my mom was as organized as Ginger was when packing these, simply throwing everything into the box instead of keeping things separated. There's everything in here from school papers to birthday cards.

"Your mom really couldn't throw some of this stuff out?" he asks, holding up a math quiz—which I got a seventy percent on.

"Honestly, I don't know why I didn't toss that out in the first place," I say, picking the paper out of his hand and tossing it in the trash. "It does bring back memories though. Remember studying for this?" I hold up a Spanish paper from our senior year. We had the same teacher that year, but during different class periods.

"Oh shit," he says, a smile brightening up his eyes as he takes it from my hands. "We sucked at Spanish, I was sure we were going to fail this. How long did we study? Two weeks?"

"A week," I correct. "But we both passed, which wouldn't have been possible if you didn't come over every night."

"It helped that you drew pictures on the flashcards. That's

how I visualized them during the test," he pauses, and I wonder if he's picturing us in my room running through flashcards like our life depended on it. "You don't want to keep this, right?" he asks, holding it over the trash can. Half of me wants to keep it, if only for the memory of that week, but instead I shake my head and let him toss it.

The birthday cards are quickly checked for any cash I might have missed before they're thrown away. Rifling through the rest of the papers, I'm confident most of them can be tossed, but I don't want to accidentally throw out something I might need. What if my birth certificate is in here and nobody realized? That's when I see a small scrap of paper that sends a warmth to my heart.

Picking it up, I read over the message before handing it to Noah. "Remember this?"

He picks his head up from the papers he's looking at and grabs the small scrap from my hand. "Is this from me?" He holds it next to his face like seeing it next to him will confirm its origin. The note doesn't say much, a "see you at school, good luck on the test" in his scribbled—almost illegible—handwriting. He used to leave me notes if he got up before me and I didn't wake up. There's probably a box of them somewhere in one of these boxes since I never threw any of them away.

"Yeah, no one else had handwriting that bad," I say, not being able to miss the opportunity to tease him. He grunts as he pokes me in my side and I let out a small shriek. When he goes to toss the note in the trash I'm quick to grab it from his hand and set it aside. His eyebrows perk up at that, and my cheeks heat, but neither of us say anything about it.

Maybe now would be a good time to bring up the other night and what happened all those years ago. Never getting closure from him has eaten away at me, keeping me up at night and creeping into my mind right before I'm about to fall asleep.

I lose my train of thought when I spot what looks like another birthday card, but with Noah's handwriting on the front, my name is the only thing on it. Did he give me a birthday card and I forgot to open it?

"What's this?" I wonder out loud, grabbing it and flipping it over to realize it's unopened. I look up from the card at Noah whose bright eyes are wide with fear and his face is pale like he saw a ghost.

"That's nothing," he says too quickly, grabbing the card from my hand before I have time to react and keep it between my fingers.

My hand follows the path through the air to try to regain possession, but I get blocked by the trash can and Noah holding it far away from me, which only makes me want it more.

"Give it back," I whine, standing and moving the trash can out of my way to step closer to him.

He's faster than me though, hopping off his stool and holding the card in the air as I reach around him for it.

"Sorry, not happening," he says, and there's no playfulness in his tone.

"Give it to me," I yell, jumping and trying to reach for it, but his arm is too high for me to reach. I can hear him suck in a breath when I end up rubbing against him while jumping. His arm comes around my waist on the last jump when my feet land unevenly and I stumble.

"It's nothing, we can toss it," he says, holding me tighter to him but not lowering his arm.

"If it's nothing, let me see it," I counter, and the pace of his heart beating faster is evident as I grip the fabric of his shirt underneath my fingers and see his pulse beating rapidly in his neck while I try to sound serious when all I want to do is climb him to get it.

We stand there forever. Him staring at me in a full Statue of Liberty position while I glare up at him.

"Fine," he finally resigns, lowering his hand and letting go of me.

I step away from him and take the card, ripping into the edge and down the crease. Noah doesn't move as I pull out the cream card with 'Thank you!' printed on the front in a fancy blue cursive font.

"What is this?" I ask, confused why he would have given me a thank you card.

"It was all my mom had at the time, it's really nothing," he says in a low voice, avoiding my eyes.

I don't let my curiosity wait too long before I open the card to a handwritten note from him. Only one side of the card is filled out, and I start reading.

> *Vi,*
>
> *I'm sorry I told you I was leaving for college tomorrow, it's actually today.*

"Noah, what is this?" I pause, unable to say anything else.

"Keep reading," he says, guiding me to sit on the stool again as he pulls his closer to sit across from me. My body listens to him as his knees hit mine and he rests his hand on top of my thigh. His touch is comforting, which is in direct contrast with the race my heart is now running. I'm scared to read whatever else this note might say. All these years I assumed he left without saying goodbye, and now that might not be true?

I realize I'm staring at his chest when he lifts his other hand to tap at the note I've got a death grip on. My eyes immediately land where I left off.

I recognize this is probably a cop out, but I couldn't handle saying this to you in person. And I couldn't keep it to myself any longer...

I'm in love with you, with everything about you. From the way your smile goes all the way up to your eyes and how you stick your tongue out when you're drawing. I've been in love with you for years, and I wanted you to know.

We're not going to be next door to each other anymore, but if you love me I want to try this. Try us.

I got a new phone to start fresh, so if loving me is something you'd like to try out, text me. The new number is 555-972-8340. If you don't text, I won't bother you again. Don't feel bad if you don't love me too. I'll never regret a moment I spent with you. You were the only thing that made high school bearable.

Love,
Noah

My heart is pounding in my ears and a drop of water falls to where his name is at the bottom of the card. I only realize it's coming from my own eyes when Noah's thumb reaches up and wipes away a tear running down my face.

The touch brings me back to reality and I look up at a blurry Noah. A blurry Noah who has been in love with me? For the past eight years I've told myself he was done with me and wanted nothing to do with me.

I'm unsure how to process this so instead of wondering to myself I say, "I never got this."

"I'm starting to realize that now," he scoffs, shaking his head. "I left it in your room before I left. I didn't think anyone was home, so I was going to leave it on your pillow. Then I heard something and panicked. I ended up tossing it toward your pillow and rushing to get out the window. I guess I tossed it too hard," he explains, rubbing his hand through the scruff along his guilty looking face.

"I thought you wanted me out of your life," I tell him, needing him to understand where my mindset has been since then.

"I thought you hated me," he says, and my heart tightens that he could ever think I could hate him.

"Do you still want to try?" I ask, moving one of my hands to rest over his. His skin is right under mine, and he flips his hand over to lock our fingers together.

"What?" he looks shocked again, but this time it's not a worried look, but a happy one. "You mean that doesn't scare you off at all?"

"No. I felt the same way about you back then, being here with you again has only brought those feelings back," I admit, not willing to tell him I love him quite yet. It's still too soon to say it, but I'm sure that's what this is.

Noah answers me with a kiss, standing and cupping my face in his hands. He wastes no time pulling my mouth to his as he hovers over me. His vanilla taste and smell are the only things I'm aware of. Before I can overthink this and stop us, I'm standing too and wrapping my arms around him as his tongue tastes every inch of my mouth, only coming up for air when it's absolutely necessary.

"I take that as a yes?" I ask when he finally stops kissing me, pulling me into a tight hug.

"It's a hell yes. I can't believe you never read it," he says, and I can hear the disbelief in his laugh.

"Me either, but I'm glad I read it now," I say, grateful I'm not going to have to sleep another long night wondering why he left me when he's loved me all along—or used to at least. I'm not sure if he's still in love with me, like I am with him, but I don't want to ask right now and ruin this perfect moment.

"Will you sleep here again?" he asks into my hair.

"Of course," I say into his chest as I hold him closer to me. There's no way I'm going to let him go again.

eighteen

NOAH

LAST NIGHT VIOLET and I fell asleep the second we crawled into my bed. She immediately curled into me and felt so right tucked to my chest. I kept waking up, worried I had dreamed everything and would find her gone. I still can't believe I spent eight years not talking to her over a misplaced card. I should have texted her, but I didn't want to overstep if she didn't want to hear from me.

Now I resemble a zombie trudging through the market with Violet. We managed to get everything we needed into two boxes, which I was able to fit on a wagon I found in the basement. I remember Ginger raving about it and how the tires were perfect for the winter. Violet follows behind the wagon, making sure the cookie warmer doesn't fall off. This morning I decided to test it one last time and it was still acting up, so now we are running late.

The market is already in full swing, with kids running around high on sugar and the promise of presents from Santa. I almost run into one because I'm staring at the map Bernice gave me with our stand circled. It's like everyone's eyes are on us as we walk by, and there's a pit of anxiety deep in my gut.

The sound of the wagon grows louder with each step until my stomach threatens to empty itself despite the lack of food in it. Finally reaching the end of the stands I see ours, stopping dead in my tracks. I hear Violet swear as she runs into the wagon, but I'm too busy taking in the disaster in front of me.

The stand is empty with a piece of printer paper taped to the front with "Gingerbreads" written on it, but it's blocked with a giant 'get out' in spray paint that covers the majority of the wood. It's exactly something my friends and I would have done in high school if we heard the rumors circulating like the ones about me. Emotion floods through me and I can't tell if I want to cry or scream, maybe both at the same time. My vision starts to blur and the air I'm breathing isn't entering my body anymore.

"Noah, take a lap. Cool down," Violet says, her hands cover my face, forcing me to look at her instead of the stand. I'm not sure when she got in front of me, but I focus on her eyes and those deep blues that I could get lost in. She's right, I need to not be here right now.

"Vi—" I try to speak, but nothing comes out.

"Listen, you know that stuff isn't true. I'm going to take care of it." Her voice is confident and determined. "Go get us some hot chocolate, okay?"

I'm only able to nod, passing the wagon off to her before I head the other way. This must've been the reason everyone was staring at us. They all knew the stand was like this and didn't bother to do a thing.

How am I supposed to prove I'm worthy if they won't give me a chance? How could Violet ever accept me when everyone else is determined to push me away? It's embarrassing to be associated with me, so why would she stay? She's probably going to take back everything from last night, and I need to prepare myself to be alone again.

I want to go back to the shop and lock the doors. This town doesn't need Gingerbreads. I don't know why I thought coming here and doing this was a good idea. I should've stayed in New York where I was fine living my unlovable life. It's not like I deserve to be loved anyway, I always find a way to ruin things like I've ruined this. Coming here only opened me up to more disappointment.

Something hot burns my hand and I realize I must've spaced out while buying hot chocolate mid-spiral. Part of me wants to leave and crawl into bed, but I can't leave Violet alone. I need to at least say goodbye this time. I notice an empty bench nearby and head there first. I need to work up the courage to go back to the stand. Maybe I could go get paint from Hanson's and paint over it, though, I'm not sure how well that will work in the cold. I could stand in front of it to hide the writing, that's always an option. Either way, I'm sure I'll have to figure it out once Violet leaves.

After several minutes of talking myself out of bad fixes to the problem, I finally calm down enough to return. There are less eyes on me this time as I weave my way through the crowd, but that doesn't mean they're all looking away. I focus on the crunch of snow and salt under my feet and try not to overanalyze every look directed my way.

Looking up from my feet, I see Violet standing behind a completely different stand. Jacob and Ava stand next to her, placing various cookies in the warmer now setup at the front of the stand. There's a blanket draped over the front covering the spray paint, and tinsel wrapped around the sides. The Gingerbreads sign she made hangs above her head, and I can't even tell this stand looked like shit.

"Stop staring and get back here," Violet calls, snapping me out of it. Her bright smile pulls me toward her, and it takes everything in me to keep myself from pulling her to me and losing myself in her lips.

There's so much going on in my head right now between whatever this is with Violet and this stand, and I'm experiencing so much more emotion in this one month than I have for the past several years. I can't believe she did all of this for me when I've given her nothing but work in return. All I can do is hand her the hot chocolate and hug her, hoping she can sense the overwhelming amount of gratitude I feel.

"Thank you," I whisper into her hat.

"Of course, now let's sell some cookies," she says, taking a sip.

The small high I had when I returned to the stand slowly fades as the night goes on and no one shows up. No one looks our way as they walk by, and mothers pull their kids in the other direction. I've been on the verge of tears all night, but I don't want to cry in public. Violet does her best to get people's attention, with no luck besides one kid who almost came over until he saw me. It's like I'm wearing a monster mask that's scaring everyone away.

By the end of the night it's our families and Sydney, my only friend in this town, that end up being our only customers, but that barely counts since those people already know me. Sydney came with the deputy, and there was definitely some tension between them. Violet asked me about it when they left, but I didn't have the energy to unpack that tonight.

She rolled her eyes at me with something about how, "Boys are useless. I'll see if Iris knows."

I didn't have any reply, too focused on how utterly stupid I must have been to think this could ever work.

I'm trying to pack all the cookies to bring them to the shop instead of leaving them here, but all I want to do is get back as fast as I can so I can cry in peace. Violet comes up behind me as I load the last of the cookies on the wagon, setting her hand on my shoulder.

"I'm so sorry," her soothing voice is a whisper, but it's not enough to fix this disaster. "Tomorrow will be better, I promise."

"It doesn't matter," I snap, mad she can't say this was a total shit show. "I'm done. Go home."

She quickly pulls her hand away from me, and I instantly regret snapping.

"I'm sorry," I say, taking a deep breath. "I just want to go home and to bed. I don't know if I want to do this tomorrow. I don't want help taking this stuff back, I need to be alone."

She nods. "Okay. Let me know if you need anything?"

"Will do," I say, and then she walks out of the stand. I feel awful, but I need some time to be alone.

nineteen

VIOLET

MY ROOM IS LIT by nothing but the digital clock on the nightstand and the glow of the street light as I welcome the darkness after such a horrible day.

Once I got home I gave my parents a recap of how the night went before getting ready for bed. They promised to come tomorrow, and bring a few of their friends with them. Part of me wanted to push back when Noah said he wanted to go home alone, but I understood the need for solitude for a while.

I want to yell at this town for being so judgmental and I want to scream at Noah for not believing in himself. He was already so dejected, I wasn't going to get anywhere with him. Hopefully by the morning he'll be open to trying again.

When my phone vibrates next to me, and I answer it so quickly without registering who is calling because I'm sure it's Noah.

"Violet? Thank God, I've been trying to reach you." Greg's shrill voice assaults my ears like nails on a chalkboard. I'm not sure how I ever thought it was sexy. Now it's only annoying.

"There's a reason I haven't been replying," I sigh into the phone.

"But, baby, I made a mistake," he pleads as my eyes roll and I gag at the pet name.

"I don't think you did," I counter.

"Please, baby, give me one more chance. Come home."

I scoff at the word 'home,' I could never think of anywhere with him as home again. Not when I feel more at home here, even if I don't fully feel like I belong yet. "I'm not doing this. You broke up with me and I realized it was the best thing to ever happen to me. Goodbye Greg," I say, ending the call without giving him a chance to reply.

I block his number and toss my phone across the bed, and now I'm fully pissed. Greg thinks he can call and tell me to come back and I'll come running? Like he didn't kick me out of our apartment without talking to me first. The audacity of some men is astounding.

That phone call was the last thing I needed after today. Yesterday ended so beautifully, but now I'm in the worst mood I've been in since I got home. I should've looked at who was calling before I answered.

The sound of the window opening makes me jump as I reach for the lamp on the nightstand to defend myself.

"I lied," Noah says without any preamble as he crawls through the window. "I don't want to be alone."

My heart drops into my stomach, heavy with sadness for him but also filled with gratitude he's here. Seeing how much he's done and people in this town still don't understand how amazing he is makes me want to go door to door and tell them about him. Placing the lamp back, I reach to pull out the second bed, but he ditches his shoes and crawls in next to me on top of the comforter. I have to move against the wall to make room for him. It used to be much easier for both of us to fit into this bed, now his large frame leaves me less room as he lays on his side next to me, our bodies touch and the heat of him warms me .

"You didn't think to call first?" I ask as he adjusts himself so his head is near my shoulder. My heartbeat picks up when he wraps his arm around my waist and pulls me to him like I'm the only thing he needs right now. His head moves to rest on my boobs and our legs intertwine around each other as his frame shrinks into me.

"Sorry, when I realized it, I didn't want to wait any longer," he admits, adjusting his head further up my body. "I can hear your heartbeat."

"You scared me," I partially lie, knowing that my heart is beating because he's wrapped around me. "How are you doing?"

He does his best to shrug in the position we're in as my hand rubs over his shoulder. "I took a shower and cried a lot, so I'm better. Feeling defeated."

"They don't know what they're missing," I tell him. "I'm still proud of you."

"You're probably the only one," he laughs.

"Tomorrow will be better. Two steps forward?"

Noah groans, burrowing closer to me like I'm still not close enough to him. "Yeah, yeah, one step back. But I don't want to think about that, I just want to sleep next to you."

I don't say anything, simply bringing my other hand to his hair and stroking it. He relaxes beneath my touch and I try to sort out everything going on in my head. Maybe he's right and we are wasting our time, maybe I should stop thinking about opening my heart up to him. But the way he makes me feel is so different from anything I ever felt with Greg. If I open my heart to Noah fully and he ends up changing his mind I don't know if I could survive another eight years of silence, but this risk might be worth the reward.

"Violet. I can't sleep with all the thinking you're doing. Talk it out with me. What's going on in your head?" He gazes at me through his lashes breaking me out of my spiral. I don't under-stand how he can understand me better than Greg ever did.

"Greg called me right before you got here," I admit, but he stays silent waiting for me to continue. "He wants to get back together."

"What do you think about that?" His eyes don't leave mine. I look away, unwilling to admit I'm scared to love him completely with him looking at me like that.

"I'm thinking about how I'm scared of the unknown. Almost like how people feel about the deep sea. With Greg, I knew what to expect. I was comfortable in our relationship, even if I didn't realize I was unhappy. Now there's this unknown being back here and I don't know if my heart is ready to take that risk of being hurt again so soon," I admit. I hope that he picks up on him being the unknown, but I don't know if he's still feeling like he wants to try this thing between us after today. I need to know he won't disappear again and change his number if things start getting serious with us.

"I don't think you need to be afraid, not when you've got a first mate to your captain," he says as his hands tighten into fists against my skin, leaning into my mention of the deep sea.

"Are you serious about that?" I counter, needing him to say more so I don't unblock Greg's number.

He sighs, pushing up and away from me which leaves his arms on either side of my waist and caging me between him. I can see his forearms flex and he twists his body to face me without falling off the bed. "You're stubborn," he glares at me, a hint of playfulness in his tone. "No, I wasn't lying when I said I wanted to try with you. I'm not going to leave you. This whole thing only works if we do it together. I can't do this alone," he tells me.

A small weight lifts from my shoulders, thankful he's not changing his mind after everything today. "That's good, I blocked Greg," I tell him so he knows I don't have any second thoughts about us either, and that I'm in if he is.

He lets out a sigh of relief and starts to lower his body to mine when there's a knock at the bedroom door.

"Honey, Dad and I are going to bed now," Mom says through the door.

"Okay, goodnight," I call, my voice breaking slightly on the last word as he hovers above me.

"Goodnight, and goodnight Noah," she says, and my head falls to the headboard. My cheeks heat and I wonder how well he can see them in the dim lighting.

"Forgot they could hear us." He laughs and lowers himself next to me.

"At least their room is on the other side of the house," I mutter, running my hands over my face, the slight coolness of my palms calming the blush on my cheeks.

"That's good," he whispers, reaching and turning my face toward him. "Because I don't want you to hold back."

His eyes darken as he stares at me and I'm back in the moment before my mom interrupted, I'm sure he was about to kiss me again. I've been craving to be with him again, but I need to draw clear lines in the sand.

"What does this mean?" I ask, pointing my finger between us.

His hand moves down my arm to my hip, leaving goosebumps in their wake. "It means you're my girlfriend. If that's okay with you," he says, moving an inch closer.

His hand on my hip moves in slow circles and I'm starting to lose the ability to talk, only able to nod in agreement.

"I also have a confession," he tells me, moving closer again. "I haven't been able to stop thinking about the other night and the way you touched yourself. I've wanted to kiss you since the first time I came over here when we were kids. At first I came over to kiss you, but I got too scared, then we became friends and I didn't want to ruin that. Now I want to keep kissing you and be the one to make you fall apart this time. If that's what you want. All you have to do is ask. Can you do that?"

His grip on my waist tightens and his fingers slip beneath the hem of my shirt, brushing against my skin. The touch sets me on fire and the ache between my thighs starts to overwhelm my senses.

"I want to be your girlfriend, and for you to kiss me again," I admit through my heavy breathing, bringing the widest smile to his face. "But most of all I want you to make me come."

His nails dig into my skin, and I arch into the touch. "As you wish," he says and brings his lips to mine.

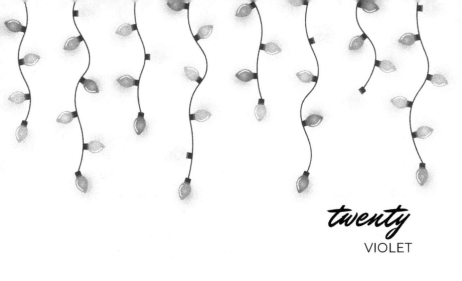

twenty

VIOLET

NOAH'S LIPS are soft as they cover mine and I'm positive I must be dreaming that I'm kissing Noah Callahan in my childhood bedroom.

He pulls me closer to him, so we are facing each other on our sides. He groans into my mouth, sliding his tongue across my lips as I open for him. The sound sends chills straight down my spine and between my legs, and it's taking everything to not climb onto his lap and give him another orgasm.

Bringing my hand to his face, I rake my nails across his jaw and he groans again. His other hand finds its way into my hair and every touch sends shockwaves through my body.

Noah pulls back, breaking the kiss, and we're both panting like we've finished a triathlon.

"My last tests were all negative, in case you wanted to know," he tells me.

"I got one after the breakup," I say, grateful I did because I didn't trust Greg didn't sleep with his coworker. "All negative too."

He groans, kissing the sensitive spot of my neck before

coming up for air. "Can I touch you?" he asks, running his fingers down my shirt and over the top of my leggings.

I gasp at the touch, involuntarily arching into it. "Only if you let me touch you," I manage to get out as I move my hand up his leg and along his inner thigh. My hand brushes against the bulge in his pants and he lets out a sharp gasp. I could feel it under me the other night, but tonight I want it in my hands.

"Fuck yeah," he says, quickly releasing me and undoing his belt. He moves at lightning speed, pulling his pants and boxers down and tossing them off the bed, leaving him in just his shirt. He grips his cock in his hand, and I can't take my eyes off it as he slowly pumps himself and squeezes at the top. "Like what you see?"

I nod, and my heartbeat is so loud now I can hear it in my ears. I reach out to touch him, but he releases his cock and stops my hand.

"Not so fast, it's your turn," he says, bringing my hand to my leggings.

I got so wrapped up in watching him I forgot I'm still fully clothed. Listening to his direction, I slip my leggings and underwear off, tossing them to join his clothes on the floor. He watches me hungrily like I watched him, stroking himself as I turn toward him.

"You have no idea how often I dreamt about this," he admits. "Sometimes after sleeping here I'd wake up early and go home to relieve myself."

"I'd do the same," I tell him, reaching over and placing my hand over his. He gasps and drops his hand, allowing me to wrap my fingers around his shaft. Rolling my thumb over the top, I spread the bead of precum collected there. His hips lift and I see his jaw tighten.

"Show me how wet you are," he growls, moving to his side again to face me.

Releasing his cock, I open my legs and bring my fingers between them. I gasp when I make contact with the wetness that's pooled and I see his cock twitch. Dipping my finger inside, Noah's mouth is on mine when I moan. His cock is hard against my leg as he gets closer and moves against me. He breaks the kiss to watch me as my thumb circles around my clit.

"Fuck, Vi," he groans. "You're so beautiful." He grabs my wrist and brings my hand to his mouth. I watch mesmerized as he sucks my finger into his mouth, swirling his tongue around the tip. "And you taste amazing." He beams at me as I lean forward and bring his mouth to mine.

He releases my wrist, and brings his fingers between my legs. Capturing my moans with his mouth, he slides his fingers through my center, coating them with my wetness.

"Fuck, you're already so wet for me. Tell me what you need," he gasps between breaths.

"Two fingers inside me," I tell him, and he listens instantly as he slips his fingers inside. "And touch my clit," I manage to say through another gasp as his thumb circles around the bundle of nerves.

Reaching down, I grab the hem of his shirt and start to lift to reveal the delicious line of hair creeping up his stomach. I'm dying to find out what he looks like shirtless now, I want to get my mouth on every part of him.

Before I can get too high he stops me. "No time, I need you to touch me," he begs, moving closer to me and increasing the pressure on my clit.

"Spit first," I instruct, releasing his shirt and bringing my hand below his mouth.

He groans, listening to me and spitting into my hand. I reach between us and take his cock in my hand as he pumps his fingers in and out of me. We're a mess of tangled limbs and quick kisses as we bring each other to the edge. He kisses along my jaw, down my neck, and up to my lips, never once breaking the rhythm with his fingers.

"I'm close," I say, gripping his cock harder.

"Can you be quiet when you come?" he growls into my ear.

I nod, unable to form a coherent yes as my orgasm approaches, worried I might moan too loud if I open my mouth.

"Good girl. Can I come on you?" he asks between kisses.

I nod again, and angle his cock more toward my leg so I won't have to change my shirt. The movement causes him to break the kiss and throw his head back. His eyes are closed and his mouth is open in ecstasy as we match each other's pace.

The second he returns his heated gaze to mine my orgasm crashes into me and he kisses me, muffling the moan that escapes from my throat. His fingers don't stop as my orgasm continues and his cock pulses under my fingers. Then, he's coming and coating my leg with his release. Slowing his fingers as I come down from the high, he breaks the kiss and drops his head to the headboard.

"Tell me why we weren't always doing this?" he laughs, looking over at me.

"Because we were stupid teenagers," I say.

"Let's never be stupid again." He runs his finger through the cum on my leg, bringing it to my mouth where I suck it off. The taste of me is still on his fingers, and mixed with the taste of him it's the most erotic thing I've ever had touch my tongue.

"Agreed," I smile at him, leaning forward for one last kiss.

twenty-one

NOAH

THIS MORNING I woke up thinking of last night and surrounded by Violet's scent. Laying tangled with her on the bed instead of the trundle seems wrong since I've never slept up here before, but it also feels like the only thing I know that's right. For starters, this mattress is one hundred times more comfortable. Either that or waking up with my girlfriend in my arms makes it seem that way. I'm finally confident in where things are headed now, at least with her. Even if today goes poorly, I'll have her by my side at the end of the night. Hopefully not in this tiny bed.

I do my best to slip out from under her so I don't wake her up. I'm searching for a piece of paper to leave her a note when she stirs awake.

"Are you leaving?" she says through a yawn.

"I need to go home and shower, plus get ready for the festival today," I tell her, squatting next to the edge of the bed.

"We're going to do it again?" she asks, hopeful I'm being serious.

"Yeah, of course. Take your time getting up, I'll handle the setup of everything. Meet me at the festival." I lean forward and push her hair off her forehead to press a light kiss there. She closes her eyes again, smiling and curling up in the sheets until only her head is visible, and she's asleep before I'm out the door.

Determined to make today a good day, I head over to my mom's, where she's in the middle of breakfast with Nick. They're surprised to see me, and Nick is quick to finish his breakfast and excuse himself to check on something, leaving me alone with my mom.

"Mom, I need your help," I tell her after we finish eating, before we get sidetracked by the usual small talk.

She stares at me and I can tell she's trying to remain calm because I hardly ever ask her for help.

"It's not bad," I reassure her. "I need you to spread the word about Gingerbreads having a stand, get people to come by today. Tell them I'll give them a discount if they mention you."

"Oh good gosh, Noah. You scared me for a second." She shakes her head, bringing her hand to her chest. "Of course I'll spread the word."

I thank her, and then I'm gone. The bounce in my step gets me to my apartment quicker than usual, and my cheeks are starting to get sore from the grin that hasn't left my face since last night.

I busy myself by eating more and showering. I want to bake more cookies for tonight, since I didn't properly store the ones we made for yesterday. In hindsight, I shouldn't have let my anger get the best of me. The cookies are probably okay to serve today, but I want to bring fresh ones for our second shot.

It might not matter though, if no one shows up again I would only be wasting more ingredients. Looking at myself in the mirror, I realize I'm about to spiral when I notice the tattoo on my chest. I mentally stop the spiral before it can get out of hand. I need help, and that's okay. I've got my people now.

Remembering the prompts of one of Ginger's letters, I make a beeline for the box. After rifling through it for a minute, I finally find the right one.

Open when you need extra encouragement

Dear Noah,

Stop sitting around and get going. Life is too short to be sitting around waiting for something to happen—make something happen!

Don't think you can?

Remember the time I couldn't figure out the new register? You wasted no time helping me and teaching me how to use it. You're capable of more than you know.

Now go!

All my love,

Ginger

The abruptness of the letter makes me laugh, and there's a small tightness in my chest as I recall the moment Ginger's referencing. She was never good with technology, which was funny then, not so much now as we drown in the paperwork she left.

Following her advice, I get up and get going.

There's a light snowfall tonight, and Violet can't stop pointing out how beautiful the snow is against the Christmas lights. I was thankful when we got to the market and the stand didn't get vandalized overnight.

Violet and I are in matching forest green sweaters, something she demanded from me after picking them up today. I obviously put up a fight, but I was ecstatic she went out and got something for me. She's wearing the red lipstick that was missing from her lips last night, and I want to pull her close and kiss her.

We don't talk any more about our new status, but my hands constantly being pulled toward her might give us away to anyone who stops by. Both of us take any chance we have to be close to the other. I take it as a good sign she's not freaked out about us. All day my thoughts have been nothing but cookies and Violet, Violet and cookies.

I'm too lost in watching her to notice a family has approached the stand and started talking to her.

"Noah, can you hand me a box?" Violet snaps me out of my thoughts.

Taking a second to understand her question, I grab a small box we brought over from the shop.

"Which ones did you want again?" she asks the tall brunette with a baby in one of her arms, and toddler holding the hand of the other.

"Coco!" the toddler shouts from below.

The woman laughs, handing the baby to her wife and pulling out her wallet. "What he said, four hot chocolate, four peppermint, and four chocolate chip please," she repeats her order and she must be joking. There's no way she could want that many cookies.

I can only watch in shock as Violet takes her money, and hands her the cookies. "Thank you, and have a lovely evening."

"No, thank you, these smell delicious. I'm so glad we stopped by," the woman says, then turns to me. "When will the storefront be open?"

Violet kicks me when I don't answer. "Hoping to be open right after the new year," I stumble over the first few words before finding my footing.

"Fantastic, we'll swing by." She smiles at me before walking away.

Meanwhile, I'm too busy standing there with my mouth open to reply to her.

"Do you need a crash course in customer service?" she teases, bumping my hip with hers.

"Did you know her?" I'm in too much shock to tease her.

"No, but it was a cute family," she says.

"So they came here because..." I trail off, uncertain how to finish that sentence.

"Because they wanted to. Don't be so surprised, you've worked hard," she says, looping her arm through mine and resting her head on my shoulder.

I laugh in response, it doesn't feel deserved or earned even though I have worked hard. I don't think it ever will. But if Ginger and Violet believe in me there must be something I'm doing right.

Doubt is soon overcome by the pure joy as more people approach the stand and buy cookies. Working with Violet is easier than I could have ever hoped for, and we fall into an easy rhythm as I package and she handles the payments. Having her next to me, now as my girlfriend, makes everything easier. We don't sell out, but it doesn't matter to me. I would have been happy if it had only been that first family. By the end of the night, we collapse into my bed, falling asleep soon after our heads hit the pillows.

twenty-two

VIOLET

IT'S BEEN one week since the first successful night at the market and I've spent every night at Noah's. With all the work of running the stand and figuring out the mess in Ginger's office we haven't had time to relax or explore our relationship more.

Our pattern of work all day and night continues each day, only to be so exhausted by the end that we fall into bed. There have been quick kisses here and there, but nothing more.

He's determined to get the shop officially open after the new year like he told our first customer, which means I need to figure out all the business stuff he didn't. After three days of searching I finally found Ginger's tax files in a folder labeled 'Boston Tea Party.'

Now I'm sitting next to him on his couch, sipping the coffee he made for us as a Christmas episode of *The Office* plays on his TV and my hand slowly moves over his tattoos. We have to get up and get moving soon, but this small moment of relaxation isn't something I want to give up right now.

"What are all these tattoos?" I ask, tracing a small waving

ghost on his forearm. I've been curious about them since I first saw him, but keep forgetting to ask.

"Most of them are silly. The ghost was a flash tattoo for Friday the 13th," he tells me, glancing to where my finger lingers on his skin.

"He's really cute," I counter. "So is this." I move my finger lower to a crescent moon wrapped in vines.

"Cute and cool. I got most of them because I thought they were cool," he laughs, shrugging and I notice his cheeks are turning pink. I don't draw attention to it though, not wanting him to get embarrassed about talking about himself and stop.

"Like this one?" I ask, moving to a geometric dragon near his wrist.

"Especially that one," he says, and his blush deepens.

Moving my fingers up his arm, I lift the sleeve of his T-shirt, surprised I haven't taken the time to explore him like this. Hopefully things will start to slow down soon and I can take my time with him. I don't want the first time I feel him inside me to be rushed at all.

Noah narrates as I trace each tattoo with a light brush of my finger, my touch leaving goosebumps scattered across his skin. Next to his ghost is another Friday the 13th special tattoo, a skeleton hand holding up a peace sign. On his bicep is a small glass of milk and chocolate chip cookies, which he said "you cannot laugh at this, it's for Ginger" and it took everything in me not to giggle. The other two hidden by his sleeve are an elephant in the same geometric style as his dragon and a skull with a bird on top, both of which he explained by saying "they're cool, I don't know."

His other arm seems more thought out, with the violet from me at his wrist leading up to various movie and television show tattoos. These include, a knife with Ghostface from *Scream*, a

Walter White silhouette from *Breaking Bad*, a skull for the pirate show *Black Sails*, and the a-frame from *Midsommer*. Hidden under his sleeve are more "because they're cool tattoos" including a cat with vines and a geometric butterfly. Going through all of them and learning more about his likes and thought process makes me want to find my old stick and poke kit. I haven't had a creative outlet in years, but now my mind is racing with new ideas for him.

"We should do something fun before the festival," I tell him once the tattoo tour is done.

"Like what?" He eyes me curiously.

"Isn't the Pet Rescue Benefit today?" I slowly smirk at him.

"I want to say yes, but I also want to say no because of that smile," he says, leaning away from me.

"Don't be afraid, we don't have to stay long, just go to support. Iris said there will be music and pets available for adoption, that could be cool," I say, trying to act cool about it. We could use a furry companion.

"Okay, that sounds like a good idea. What time does it start?" he asks.

"I think four, so we can get stuff ready for tonight first and then go," I say cheerfully.

"Perfect, but let's watch another episode first," he says, pulling me closer to him.

Noah whines as I pull him further into the crowd. It's bigger than I expected with the festival still going on, but it seems like everyone had the same idea we did. Several people who stopped at the stand last night wave as we pass them, and my heartstrings tighten seeing more people positively acknowledge Noah.

"We only have to stay for a little while, then we'll go to the festival," I reassure him.

His grunt is the only reply I get, but he keeps following me. I saw my destination the moment we got here, the sounds of barks and meows pointing me in the right direction. There are volunteers everywhere and a banner reads 'Adopt an Evergreen Lake Pet Today!'

"Violet," he chastises from behind me, and he pulls my arm. "Why are you going toward the animals?"

"Noah," I return, elongating the second part of his name. "What kind of town members would we be if we didn't say hi to the cats and dogs?"

"The regular kind?" he grunts.

"You'll be fine, I only want to say hi quickly," I tell him.

I hear him whisper, "Famous last words," right as we reach the table. One of the volunteers, Avery, greets us and I take note of the they/them pronouns on their name tag.

They go through their elevator pitch of all the animals available and some information about the event. I'm half listening, distracted by a group gossiping next to us. I accidentally tune Avery out when I hear Noah's friend Sydney's name come up. I make out something about her and that deputy she was with earlier this month, but Noah is closer than me.

I elbow Noah who is being less subtle, staring directly in the direction of the gossiping crew. He whips his head toward me with a raise of his eyebrow, which I return with a raise of mine. He nods once in a silent "discuss later" and then we are focusing on the end of Avery's sales pitch.

They point over to a large crate of cuddling cats next to us, all of whom are tangled in each other, and a black one pops their head up to look at me.

I wave and its eyes follow the movement of my hand, standing and stepping over the other cats to come to the edge of the crate. Reaching out I put my fingers up to the edge so they can smell me. Their eyes are curious as they push their nose through the metal slots.

"That's Simon, he's about two years old," Avery tells us. "Full disclosure, he's been returned to the rescue a few times now."

My heart instantly sinks as the cat tries to lick my fingers, his tongue rough. "That's awful, why was he returned?" I ask.

"They always said he wasn't a good fit, but honestly people don't like black cats so I'm not surprised," they tell us.

"That's stupid," Noah grunts.

"You should adopt him," I turn to Noah. "He matches you."

"You adopt him," he volleys.

"And keep him where? I don't have a permanent place to live," I remind him.

"Yeah, I can't let you adopt a pet without a place to live," Avery says, running their hand along the back of their neck.

"I can't, we have to go to the festival and work the stand," Noah says. "I'm sure Bernice is waiting for any opportunity to shut my stand down."

"Simon is actually a fairly good outdoor cat, he loves the leash. And the festival has a pets welcome policy," they tell us, picking up a leash from the table.

I look over at Simon who is sitting staring at us and then to Noah, who glares at me like he is getting ready to kill me.

"Can I hold him?" I ask, returning my attention to Simon.

"Sure thing." Avery opens the crate, hooking the leash to the top of Simon's harness. He comes willingly out onto the table as the volunteer ensures no other cats escape. Handing over the leash to me, Simon moves right in front of me. I let him smell my hand again before reaching underneath his belly to pick him up. Supporting his butt with my other arm, I pull him close to me and feel him purring before I hear it. He nuzzles his head into my chest and if my heart could melt it would.

I peer over at Noah, putting on my best pouting face and big eyes. But he's already grabbing one of the clipboards from the table to fill out an adoption form.

"You have to pay the fee," he tells me, keeping his eyes on the form.

"Deal," I squeal, jumping in place and holding Simon tighter to me.

When he's done filling out the form, I pass him Simon so I can grab my wallet out from my deep coat pockets. I watch him from the corner of my eye as he fumbles with the leash and adjusts Simon in his arms. Simon doesn't stop purring, kneading his paws on his forearm and looking at him like he hung the moon.

The blackness of the cat perfectly compliments Noah's dark outfit and beanie, with his dark hair sticking out from under it. They look like father and son, if that was a possibility. He reaches and scratches Simon's chin, and I can see the grin he's failing to hide.

He unzips his coat, tucking Simon in and keeping his arm in front of his chest to support him. Simon's head peeks out of the center of Noah's chest and it takes everything in me to not say anything in case I blow this moment.

Avery tells us all about Simon's eating habits, likes, and dislikes. We get a folder of his information, and the number of the local vet to make an appointment. They give us a small sweater for Simon so he won't get cold, but Noah doesn't take him out of his coat. We're well over the hour I said we would be here, and I've barely paid attention to the music being played.

"To the festival?" he asks, Simon still tucked close to him. I have a feeling I'm not going to get to hold him for a while.

"Do you want to put him in the carrier?" I ask, holding up the small carrier we received.

"No, I'm all set," he clenches his jaw, fighting a smile and I roll my eyes at him. He leads us out of the benefit, and I notice several people looking and pointing our way as they smile at the sight of Noah with Simon.

twenty-three

NOAH

I'LL NEVER TELL Violet this, but adopting Simon has to be my second favorite thing to happen this month. The first being when she arrived in that dive bar. For the last two nights, we've brought Simon to the festival with us, where he perches on a chair specifically designed for him. He's been a hit in his red plaid sweater, helping us to sell the most cookies we've ever sold.

I was nervous Bernice would come over and say having him at the stand was a health hazard, but I didn't see her at all. I wasn't joking when I said I thought she was waiting for me to mess something up and take the stand away. I'm still unsure if the older members of this town have accepted me like the younger adults have started to.

Yesterday, we went to the pet store and picked up extra toys and a cat tree. It's been lightly snowing since then, and he hasn't left the window. He's sitting upstairs in the apartment now as Violet and I get ready for the cookie decorating contest. Tomorrow is Christmas Eve and I'm stressed about baking so many sugar cookies for the event. It's my last chance to show the older members I can do this and won't ruin their Christmas festival. In theory it should be fine, but I'm never that lucky.

"Um Noah?" Violet calls from the front of the shop where she went to check her phone. It's been charging out there so it doesn't get anything on it. With her luck she would drop it right into the batter.

"What?" I call, sliding another batch of cookies in the oven.

The kitchen door swings open, and her head pops out. Her hair is in a messy bun on top of her head, and she's learned to wear anything besides black when we're baking. Her white tank has some dough on it, and I take a mental note to order her an apron because she's going to end up ruining all her clothes if I don't.

"So my mom texted me and it sounds like the snow isn't stopping anytime soon," she tells me, holding up her phone. I can hear a hint of concern in her voice and my heart starts to beat faster.

"How bad?" I ask, my stomach dropping anticipating her answer.

"Bad. Come look," she says, disappearing into the front.

I follow her, pushing through the door and making a beeline straight for the covered windows. Lifting one of the newspapers away, I see there's already three feet of snow minimum.

"My mom says they're talking about canceling the festival tomorrow if it keeps going like this. There's talk of telling people not to drive," she says behind me, almost so low I can't hear her.

The room is getting smaller and the only thing I can hear is my own heart attempting to escape my chest.

"Are you okay?" I hear her ask, and there's a light touch on my shoulder.

Pushing her hand off my shoulder, my feet take over and move into the kitchen. I hear the door hit the wall as I enter, and she's yelling something behind me. The kitchen is a mess, different stages of baking scattered around, and I take my anger out on the first batch of cookies I see. I crumble a cookie in my fist, and the warmth of it spreads across my palm before I pound my fists on the table, causing some of the cookies on the cooling rack to fall to the floor.

"Noah, it's going to be okay," Violet says, coming up next to me and resting her hand on my back.

"If there's no festival tomorrow, my final chance to show this town I'm not worthless before opening is gone." I turn toward her, and my throat feels like it's closing in on itself as water starts to blur my vision. "These people are never going to let me hire anyone. I don't know why I tried, this was all a big mistake."

"I think—" she starts, but I'm too upset to let her get a word in.

"It's fine. It's fine. Everything is fine. No big deal. Just go home. I'm done baking if there's no point. Maybe I won't open at all. Why would I bother, right? Right. So go home, see your family for Christmas Eve tomorrow." By the time I've finally finished my spiral, I'm standing at the back door and turning one last time before going upstairs. "Bye, Violet."

I don't wait to hear her response before I'm running up the stairs and into my apartment. Simon is right where I guessed he would be, staring out the window on his cat tree. I shed my pants and dirty shirt, wanting no trace of baking left on me. I want to curl up and do nothing, cry myself to sleep and forget everything.

My bed is warm when I pull the covers over my head, and I hear a small chirp and pressure by my feet. Popping my head out, I see Simon has joined me. He steps over my legs and nuzzles my face, moving to get beneath the covers with me.

I lift them up, allowing him the room to plop against my chest and roll over. His purring fills the room and I instantly feel better with him next to me.

I pet him until I start to doze off as my heart rate slows. My mind replays what happened over and over again. The furrow of Violet's eyebrows said she wanted to kill me, and instead of talking things out I ran away.

Wait.

What the fuck am I doing?

My eyes spring open, and Simon grunts when I stop petting him. Throwing the cover off of us, I stumble as I jump out of bed in search of clothes. I put on the nearest pair of sweatpants and a long-sleeved shirt. Violet is probably already home by now, but maybe she's still close.

Simon runs out of the room, and I follow him. Right as I cross the threshold into the hallway I run into something. No— not something. Violet.

"Vi?" I ask, stunned to see her, and to have almost knocked her over. My hands are wrapped around her biceps and she's still dressed in the same outfit from earlier.

"Present," she rolls her eyes at me. "Are you done throwing your temper tantrum?" she says, lovingly but also hitting me right where I need it.

I drop my head, releasing my grip on her. "Yes. You didn't leave?" I look at her, arms crossed and shoulders straight.

"I told you the snow was bad, I'm not sure where you thought I was going," she tells me. "Plus, who was going to hug you once you stopped throwing your pity party?"

"I'm sorry," I confess.

"I know," she says, opening her arms for me. "But you need to stop running away."

"I know." I don't hesitate as I step forward into them. Her plum and floral scent surrounds me and her nails rake along my back and into my hair as I rest my head on her shoulder. I let the disappointment consume me, and there's no stopping the tears that fall out and onto her shoulder.

twenty-four

VIOLET

I STOOD in the hallway with Noah for twenty minutes, letting him get it all out before asking if he had enough blankets to build a fort. He looked at me confused, but led me to his closet with extra blankets and sheets.

Now, Christmas music plays from Ginger's record player as he brings up a box of twinkle lights from the basement.

"You were right," he says with a roll of his eyes. "There was a box of lights in the basement."

"Of course I was right, Ginger wouldn't have tossed those," I say, satisfied I was correct when I thought I saw a box earlier and hopeful once we plug them in and see they still work.

"Want to tell me what your plan is here?" he asks, setting the box next to the blankets and chairs I've moved from the table to the middle of the living room.

"We're going to make a fort," I say cheerily, standing tall and placing my hands on my hips.

This doesn't get the reaction I was hoping for. Instead of an excited response and something to cheer him up he only furrows his eyebrows and rubs the back of his neck.

"What? You don't like the idea?" I ask, dropping my hands from my waist.

"I've actually never built one before," he admits to the floor, slowly looking at me to where my mouth is hung wide open at his confession.

"Noah. Callahan," I emphasize each syllable of his name. "You've lived on this earth for twenty six years and have never once experienced the joy of laying on the floor under a fort of blankets?" A ping of sadness tugs on my heart at the thought. I spent countless hours building forts in the living room with my sister. With our age difference, when she first went away to college it became a tradition to build one and have a sleepover the first night she would come home in between each semester.

"I never had anyone to build them with." He shrugs, leaning against one of the chairs in the room.

"Well, that ends tonight. Now you have me, and Simon, but he won't be much help. He can supervise." I gesture over to Simon who is in the middle of licking his ass on the cat tree.

"Sounds good, tell me what to do, boss," he says, standing straight and giving me a salute. My stomach flutters at the thought of being the one who gets to boss him around, since he's spent the past few weeks teaching me what to do. Now I finally get to teach him a few things.

Noah turns out to be a great listener, and his reflexes really showed whenever I tripped over the blankets and almost sent the whole thing crashing down. I taught him how to set up the chairs for optional space inside the fort, with the chairs facing backward. When he got worried laying inside wasn't going to be comfortable I assured him it would. With a combination of other blankets and the comforter from his bed, his skepticism quickly diminished.

The final step of stringing up the lights is the trickiest, since there needs to be optimal lighting inside the fort, but draping them right over the blankets is a fire hazard.

"Up one more inch," I tell Noah, whose scent surrounds me as I stand under him and watch him lift the lights higher on the wall.

"Better?" he asks, pausing and keeping the lights in place.

"Perfect." I smile at him, ripping off a piece of tape and handing it to him so he can secure the lights. "Now the best part"—he raises one eyebrow at me—"we get to go inside." His expression darkens and my heartbeat becomes more apparent in my ears.

"Wait, I have one more thing to do before we relax," I tell him, holding up one finger and ditching the tape in the kitchen. He eyes me curiously and follows me toward the front of the apartment. "I also saw some stuff in the basement we need to bring up, that's how I knew about the lights," I tell him, leaving the apartment and down the stairs.

"What stuff?" he asks, and I can envision the confused expression on his face behind me.

"Window decorating stuff. Better late than never, right? I was thinking we could do them since we're stuck here?" I tell him.

He sighs and says, "Sure, why not?"

The squeal of excitement that leaves me startles him, and thankfully causes him to laugh as he gestures toward the door. I lead us to the basement where we both grab boxes before heading through the kitchen, that I cleaned while he was upstairs, and into the shop's front area.

Flipping on the lights, I walk to the newspaper covered windows.

"Would you like to do the honors?" I spin toward him, holding the corner of one of the papers.

He smirks at me, and my stomach does a tumble, before he

meets me at the window. His large hand covers mine, and it's warm from his skin but cold from the glass.

"Together?" he asks.

"Together," I agree as we rip off the first piece.

"Holy shit," he says as we both gape at the scene behind the glass. The snow is still coming down, and the visibility on the street is minimal. The sun has long set and I can see the lights of various businesses through the darkness, but no movement. There has to be at least five feet of snow, and I have no doubt it could get taller than me.

"Well, we're definitely stuck for Christmas." I laugh, pulling another piece of newspaper off the glass.

It doesn't take us long to clean off the windows, but my fingers are getting colder the longer we stay near the window. Pulling out all the decorations has caused us to sneeze and cough due to all the dust they've collected.

Noah tells me stories about various different decorations. One year Ginger took the window chalk markers away from him for trying to draw penises. Then Sydney was banned from helping when she kept moving the reindeer stickers into the suggestive positions. Half of the decorations are unusable because of their old age, but we manage to get something on all the windows.

We step back to take in our masterpiece, and he drapes his arm over my shoulder, pulling me close. It's lit by the snow and lights, and my 'Opening Soon' might be backward to us but it's beautiful.

A sense of accomplishment fills my chest that I haven't felt in months, and I'm suddenly grateful for all the work Ginger left behind for us to pick up. With him by my side and I've found a purpose I didn't know I had. Like everything is finally right where it needs to be.

"We make a pretty good team, don't we?" he asks, pulling me from my train of thought.

"We do," I smile at him. "But we need to clean up," I say, pointing to the dust that covers both of us from head to toe.

He smirks, and I can see the mischief in his eyes. "You put these boxes in the basement and then wait maybe two more minutes and meet me upstairs," he says before disappearing into the kitchen and running upstairs.

Anticipation starts to flood my veins as I gather the boxes together and head to the basement.

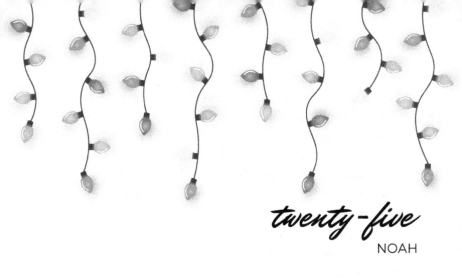

twenty-five

NOAH

"NOAH?" I hear Violet call from the hallway.

"In here," I yell, sinking below the bubbles so she can't see my chest yet. Soon though.

She's in the doorway of the bathroom a second later, frozen when she sees me. The second I had this idea I ran upstairs so fast, filling the tub and finding the bottle of bubble bath. I'm finally ready to let her in and I hope what I'm about to reveal doesn't send her running for the mountains.

"Join me?" I ask, reaching out over the tub.

She surveys the room, from the folded towels on the toilet and my clothes scattered around the floor. I didn't have time to find a candle before I heard her coming up the stairs. She doesn't say anything as she steps in and closes the door behind her. My pulse races when she reaches for the button of her jeans, slowly undoing them and sliding them down her legs.

Memories of us in her bed come to the front of my mind, and how she tightened around my fingers as she came. How I want to feel that again, and so much more. I can see the violet on her thigh from that night she gave me my first tattoo, and I want to jump out and bite it. There's more tattoos sprinkling

159

her skin that I didn't notice from our night together. A half sun and moon decorates her hip, surrounded by smaller stars.

My gaze travels up her body as she grabs the bottom of her shirt and lifts up. At the first peek of skin, I realize this is going to be the first time I've seen her like this. Does she have more tattoos that have been hidden by clothes this entire time?

All the breath leaves my lungs when my eyes land on the space between her breasts. An intricate design of lines and flowers disappear behind a sports bra, and my dick grows harder in the water. I'm not going to be able to keep my hands off her for much longer.

She moves to grab her bra, but stops to put her hair up. I let out a groan and sink further into the tub, running my hands along my face.

She giggles, and the warmth of the sound fills me. "Impatient much?" she teases.

"If you wanted to move faster and get in here, I wouldn't be against it," I laugh through my hands, peeking at her.

"Okay, fine, fine," she says as she hooks her thumbs in her underwear to slide them down her legs. They're a simple black cheeky pair, and I watch as they join my boxers next to her. Finally, she pulls her sports bra off. Her tattoo stops right between her breasts, and I can see her nipples are pebbled. I can't help the small moan that escapes my lips at the sight of her standing naked in my bathroom.

"Please, Vi," I beg, reaching my hand out to her. I do my best to help her into the tub without breaking the surface. She squeals when her toes dip into the hot water, and I'm worried I made it too hot before she finally steps into the tub. Luckily, it's big enough for both of us, and she settles in across from me. There's a second of awkwardness as she tries to figure out where to put her feet before I grab both of them and set them in my lap.

She gasps when one brushes against my hard cock, and I moan at the brief contact before she settles on my thigh.

"There's a loofa behind you," I tell her, pointing to the small shelf in the corner. Reaching behind her, she grabs it and adds some soap. I watch as she lathers herself in suds, making sure to keep her hair dry. I rub her feet beneath the water, running my hand along her shins every so often. The goosebumps on her legs are prickly underneath my fingertips and my balls tighten.

"Your turn?" she asks, holding the loofa out to me, still covered in suds.

This is the moment of truth. I'm fully aware Violet hasn't seen my bare chest, and that I've been hiding it from her. I reach up and grab her hand, pulling her closer to me. She gasps as she settles over my legs. Hers are now open and spread over mine so she's straddling me and I'm aware of how easily it would be to let her recreate our moment on the couch. I push back instead and into a better position for her to help me, my nipples tightening when they hit the cool air and my heart picks up speed like it's going to run away.

I'm watching her eyes as she takes in the tattoo spread across the left side of my chest, over my heart.

"Noah," she sighs, barely audible over the pounding of my heart as she reaches to trace the edges of the bouquet of violets. Her touch is like a fire on my skin as I wait for her to say anything about the silent confession inked in me. When I think she's about to say something, I see her eyes grow wider when she notices the tattoo over my clavicle. It's smaller than the violets, but still damming, with two footprints moving forward, and one moving back. "Noah," she breathily sighs again.

She continues to run her fingers along the lines, from my shoulder down to the violets, her touching lingering over my nipple. The pleasure shoots straight to my dick and my hands grab her waist, pulling her flush against me. Her center rubs along my shaft and my head falls against the wall. She gasps at the contact as my fingers dig into her waist, keeping her still.

"How long have you had these?" she whispers as the loofa glides over my chest.

Taking a deep breath, I lift my head to look at her. "Just under eight years."

Her movements still for only a second before she continues to wash me, moving down my arm. She's refusing to meet my eyes, but I can see the small upturn of the corner of her mouth. "Did you see my rib one?" she asks, finally glancing at me through her lashes as she washes around my wrist. "Or were you too busy looking at this one?" One hand leaves the loofa, her finger slowly dragging down her chest. I watch, memorized by the suds trailing after her finger. I hardly register when she reaches under my chin and tilts my head up to look at her. "Well?"

"No," my answer comes out jagged, and I have to clear my throat to get it back to normal. "Which side?" I ask, moving my hands up her sides, hoping to feel the slight rise of the ink on her skin without having to take my eyes off hers.

"Left side," she tells me, nodding to the area. The second she does I feel the smallest change in her skin, running my thumb over the long tattoo stretching from under her breast to her side. I don't know how I didn't notice it before. Violet drops her head at my touch, letting out a long sigh and moving her hips in the slightest so our centers rub together.

The pressure builds at the base of my spine and I do my best to not encourage her before I get to see this tattoo. I don't want to rush this moment with sex, I need to know if she's about to confess something to me as well. Removing my finger, I tilt my head to see the small cursive font spread across her skin. Black and a bit faded, I can tell it's older than her sternum one. Reading the phrase makes my heart stop before the pounding in my ears continues. 'Two steps forward, one step back' stares at me in my own handwriting. A matching sentiment to the tattoo on my clavicle.

"Vi, how long have you had this?" I ask, looking at her, but I'm already certain of the answer.

"Just under eight years," she admits, abandoning the loofa completely and resting her hands on my shoulders.

"How'd you get this?" I ask running my thumb over my handwriting that's been on her body for years. Thinking about all the times she's touched it and thought of me, how she's had me with her all these years.

"One of your notes," she tells me. "I kept every single one." I think back to all the boxes we still have to go through, and now I'm determined to find the rest of those notes. Her hands move up my neck to my jaw, cupping my face. "It's always been you," she whispers.

My body takes over as I pull her close to me and our mouths fuse together. Water splashes out of the tub as I open my mouth for her, letting her take control. Her nails rake into my hair and keep me close to her as she explores my mouth. I meet her tongue with my own, her sweet taste better than anything I can imagine. Wrapping my arms around her, I stand in the tub as her legs meet behind my back.

"Don't slip," she teases, breaking the kiss and biting my lip.

"Wouldn't dream of it," I say, stepping out of the tub. My foot slips for a millisecond before I right myself on the mat.

"Noah!" Violet screeches, laughing as she moves to kissing my neck. I hike her up higher on my body, to avoid her brushing against my cock that's begging for any kind of release. She yelps, but doesn't stop her mouth as she moves to suck on my earlobe.

I reluctantly remove one arm from her skin to grab the towel. "Dry first," I say, tossing one over her back. She huffs and stops kissing me as I run the dry fabric up and down her arms. My skin instantly misses the warmth of her mouth, but I know it won't be long until it's back on me.

"Bedroom?" she asks, her voice desperate and her eyes hungry.

"Bedroom," I agree, holding her tighter and leading us out of the bathroom.

twenty-six

VIOLET

THE MOMENT we got into the bedroom Noah dropped me onto the bed and disappeared, shouting, "Be right back."

Now, I'm sitting on his bed wrapped in my towel because his comforter is still out in the fort. I'm still in shock over his tattoos. I'm not surprised though, and now that I think about it things are starting to make sense. Like how when I came into his apartment that first night I found him sleeping naked. But when I started sleeping over he suddenly found his clothes. He wasn't trying to make me comfortable, he was hiding the beautiful bouquet on his chest. A bouquet I want to lick and bite.

Noah's been gone for several minutes before he jogs into the bedroom. His towel is hung in all the right spots for me to admire the way his hips create a perfect V to where he's holding it in place, the dusting of hair leading down to where I want to touch him.

"Take this," he says out of breath, handing me an envelope. I start to flip it over, until he yells at me. "Not yet. Wait until I'm gone."

"This is weird," I tell him, furrowing my brow.

"I know. Trust me. I'm going to go lay down in the fort. You read that, and if you like what it says, come join me. If you don't"—he pauses to rake his free hand through his hair—"stay in here and let's pretend this never happened. Deal?"

"Noah, we already agreed to try this. What does this say?" I ask cautiously, trying not to flip it over like he said.

"Consider this your last get out of jail free card, and I don't know," he says.

"You don't know? What do you mean you don't know?" I'm starting to get concerned now, and I'm unsure what's going on. I hate how he keeps attempting to push me away, like I'm lying about wanting to be with him.

"Trust. Me," he says, emphasizing each word before kissing my forehead and leaving the bedroom.

I look at the envelope in my hand. It's old and battered, yellowing slightly with age. I'm uncertain what could be in here that would make me want to forget what we've finally started and walk away. I've waited so long to be with him, I don't think anything could stop me.

Taking a deep breath, I finally stop stalling and flip over the envelope. The front only has one sentence in handwriting that I recognize right away from the papers at Gingerbreads.

Give to the person you fall in love with

Opening the envelope, I slowly pull out the paper inside and start reading.

Dearest Violet,
To start, I apologize if you're not Violet. This letter might be awkward for you to read. I can only assume if you're not Violet that she must be dead, in which case, please help Noah heal.

Anyway, Violet, I'm glad to see Noah finally figured things out. I wanted to let you know he never stopped talking about you. No matter what we were doing, he always found a way to bring you up. Whether it would be something you liked or something you said, he was always talking about you.

I tried to push him to ask you to prom, but maybe I wasn't pushy enough. I was so sad when you both left town, but I always knew you would find your way back to each other. Soulmates always do.

The only thing I ask of you is don't break his heart. He might act all tough, but we both know what's hidden under his surface.

In return, if he ever breaks your heart - call Carl from the morgue. He'll be able to help you out.

Wishing you both the best. I hope you grow old together and never lose sight of the most important thing. Your love. For each other.

All my love & happiness,
Ginger

My vision is blurry as I read the last line and a tear stains the bottom of the letter. I can't believe Ginger knew all this time. I wish Noah had listened to her. I wish we hadn't been so stupid. I wish neither of us had ever left this town.

A rush of urgency comes over me as I drop the letter on the bed and run out of the room, leaving the towel behind me as well. Goosebumps cover my skin from the cold, but I don't care. My heart is pounding as I reach the living room, only lit by the twinkling lights strung over the fort.

Dropping to my knees at the entrance I see Noah laying against pillows, a blanket spread across his lap. He's gazing at me with all the hope in the world, and it takes everything in me to not jump into his lap. He pushes off the ground, arms flexing and distracting me before I put one finger in the air. He freezes, arms straining to keep himself up.

"You love me? Like love-love me?" I ask, needing to hear the words from his lips.

"I love-love you." He nods. "I've never not loved you," he tells me, sitting up fully inside the fort. Leaning forward, he reaches out his hand to me like he did in the bathroom. A silent invitation to join him. My body takes over as my brain processes what's happening, and then I'm sitting by his side.

His warm vanilla scent fills the inside of the fort, and the lights outside shine through the sheets enough to illuminate him in the most beautifully maddening gold.

"Are you going to say anything?" he asks, squeezing my hand.

"I love you too. My heart has always belonged to you, Noah," I tell him, guiding his hand to rest over my heart. It feels like my chest can barely contain it.

He mirrors me, bringing my free hand to rest over his tattoo. My fingertips try to memorize the raised lines there as his heart beats, moving in sync with mine.

I'm not sure who leans forward first, but one second I'm looking into his eyes and the next his lips are on mine.

twenty-seven

VIOLET

KISSING NOAH IS QUICKLY BECOMING one of my new favorite activities. I don't have to think about it all. With Greg I was always wondering if I was doing it right. Was I using too much tongue? Was I too aggressive? Not aggressive enough?

Not with Noah, though.

With him, it's like a carefully planned dance we already know the choreography to. Our bodies understand how to move together without direction. Anywhere he touches me ignites a fire inside me, and every swipe of my fingers across his body elicits a moan from deep in his throat that makes wetness pool between my legs.

He moves me to my back, the blanket over his lap falling away to reveal his hard cock. I move to reach for it, but his hands are fast to grab mine and pin them over my head with a hum. I watch mesmerized as he lowers his head to my chest, one hand cupping my breast. I arch into the touch as he trails kisses down my sternum, licking the intricate design there. I anticipate his mouth on my nipple, but his kisses sprinkle the skin beneath my breast and find their way to the writing on my ribs. He traces the lines with his tongue as he finally lets go of the hand above my head, guiding my fingers to tangle in his hair.

I rake my nails along his scalp, earning a groan from him as he continues to mark every part of my body with his mouth. Slowly, he lowers himself, finding the stars on my hip. I tug on his hair to guide him lower, but he ignores me. Instead his hot breath is the only sensation I'm aware of between my legs when he moves his attention to the violet on my thigh. My first tattoo; *our* first tattoo. My legs fall open to make room for him as he sucks at the faded ink, and I think I might be able to come from only the sensation of Noah exploring the designs across my body with such care and hunger.

Right when I give up all hope of his mouth between my legs, his kisses trail to my pelvis, nipping and earning a gasp from me.

He lifts his head to look at me through his lashes, hands so tight on my hips that he might end up leaving bruises. "You have no idea how long I've thought about the way you'd taste on my tongue," he admits, kissing everywhere but where I need him most. His hot breath makes me arch closer to his mouth, seeking the feeling of him on me.

"This isn't fair," I gasp, looking away from him. "I want to taste you too."

"Give me one second," he chuckles, finally lowering his mouth to me. He wastes no time spreading me open with his tongue, finding my clit and sucking it into his mouth.

"Fuck, fuck, fuck," is all I can manage as my hips rock into his face. But I'm determined to do this together. Lifting my legs and his head, I pull him to me and flip us over. Noah stares at me with a smirk that I've been aching to kiss off his face for years. Lowering, I taste myself as I kiss him quickly, making sure to not lower myself fully and risk getting distracted.

He watches me with hungry eyes as I climb off him, readjusting myself so my legs bracket his head. He helps guide me into the right position, grabbing my hips and moving his body to fit between me. Leaning forward, I brace myself on the comforter with one hand and take his cock in my other.

His hips instantly push into my hand as he pulls my center to his face. I moan when he continues right where he left off, zeroing in on my clit with his tongue. Trying to keep myself from falling on him I wrap my mouth around the head of his cock. He groans against me and the taste of him on my tongue is better than anything I could have imagined.

I take my time exploring where he's leaking for me, slowly teasing him with short kisses and licks. My hand moves slowly up and down his shaft, keeping him right where I want him. After he nips at my thigh a few times, I finally take him fully into my mouth. Picking up my pace, I hum as his fingers dig into my hips.

"You have to stop if you want me to fuck you," he gasps between licks.

"Are you going—"

"I can't stop," he interrupts me, holding my body closer to his face and fucking me with his tongue. The orgasm builds as he licks to my clit and sucks as I rest my face on his thigh, fully succumbing to the sensation of him giving me pleasure.

"I'm going to—" I barely get out as he hums and doesn't slow his pace. The orgasm crashes into me, my hips rocking against his face as he takes his time working me through the shocks.

There's no moment to recover before Noah takes his mouth off me and flips us over. He grabs a condom from the edge of the fort, narrowly avoiding the roof and having this whole thing collapse on top of us.

I adjust myself among the scattered pillows and blankets, watching as he rolls the condom down his length.

"You're good to do this?" he asks, checking in as he kneels between my legs.

"Yes, more than you know." I smile at him, reaching for his hand and pulling him over me.

Our tongues tangle, the tastes of us mixing together. He runs his cock through my wetness before pushing into me slowly. I lift my hips to encourage him to keep going, taking him deeper inside me, until the sensation of him fully surrounding me is all I can think about.

Once he's fully seated, he wastes no time pumping into me while keeping his mouth on mine. His arms flex on either side of my head, and I can't help but run my hands over his inked skin.

"I'm not going to last long," he tells me between kisses.

"Good." I pause to kiss him harder. "Come for me, Noah," I demand, nipping his lip.

He thrusts three more times before he cries out in ecstasy, spilling into the condom inside of me. His head drops to my shoulder as he pants, and his heartbeat pounds against my chest. Finally turning his head, he kisses my cheek once before slipping out of me and pulling me into his arms.

"I love you so much, Violet. Merry Christmas," he says, resting his chin on the top of my head.

"Merry Christmas, Noah. I love you too," I tell him, laying a kiss on the bouquet on his chest.

twenty-eight

NOAH

WAKING up this morning with Violet's naked body pressed against mine felt like a dream, but seeing her wearing nothing but my shirt as she sips a coffee and sports a messy bun might be better. She looks relaxed and deliriously happy and content. I can see a hickey on her neck peeking out from under my shirt, and one on her thigh when she readjusts her legs under her.

I'm about to take her coffee away from her and have my way with her again but the ring of her phone stops me.

"Shit, where's my phone?" Her eyes widen as she springs off the couch, coffee spilling out over the rim of the mug.

"End table," I tell her. "I plugged it in for you last night." I try not to laugh at her as she scrambles for it before it stops ringing. I reach into the fort to grab my comforter, tossing it her way as she settles on the opposite end of the couch. She pulls it over her legs, handing me her coffee in the process before she swipes her phone to answer.

"Violet! Are you alive?" Her mom's voice comes alive through the phone.

"Mom, if I wasn't would you be able to see me?" She rolls her eyes and waves at the screen with her free hand.

"Take the phone away from your ear and look at the screen," Iris chimes in.

"Right, there you are. Are you safe?" her mom asks.

This morning we woke up to several more feet of snow. Everyone is snowed in, so it's good they canceled the festival. There's a makeup day scheduled for New Year's Eve, which gives us plenty of time to do other things.

"All safe, I'm with Noah," she says, spinning herself and the camera around to show me. My body heats at the awareness of how shirtless I am, and the view of me on her phone only gets more damning when I notice the hickeys all over my chest from when she explored it with her mouth. Violet seems to notice the same thing I do when she quickly whips around and almost falls off the couch before I catch her.

"With Noah, are you?" I hear the accusation in Iris's tone, but before Violet can respond her mom interjects.

"Stay there, Christmas is canceled tomorrow," she tells them. "It's too snowy to leave, I don't want either of you risking it for a day on the calendar."

"But Mom," Iris starts.

"No, no fighting. We will do a makeup Christmas when this is all cleared up," she says. "Do either of you need anything?"

"If we do, how are you going to get it to us? I don't want either of you leaving either," Violet argues.

"I saw on Facebook that Deputy Dennis is helping folks out, look out your window he might be out there," she says as Violet glances at me and points to the window.

I follow the silent cue, petting Simon on his tree as I look out the window. Just like her mom said, I see the deputy shoveling paths. It reminds me to check in on Sydney. After the pet benefit Violet got the scoop from Iris—apparently Sydney and the deputy had something going on. It seems that might not be a thing anymore based on whispers Iris has heard. I checked in on her the other day, bringing her some cookies, in case she needed anything. She was clearly sad, but didn't want to talk about it. I should start putting more of an effort in with her since I haven't, and my guilt lingers about that.

Violet is still talking to her family, and I settle on the couch, sticking my cold feet under her blanket with a small yelp from her when I touch her skin.

"What's on your neck, Vi?" Iris asks once their mom is done talking about the plan for the next week.

Her face flushes bright red and I try not to laugh when she pulls the blanket to her chin and yells, "Nothing. I'll talk to you later, love you and Merry Christmas." Then she ends the call and tosses her phone between us, burying her face in her hands.

"I should not have answered that call with the video on," she mumbles into her hands.

"Yeah, maybe not," I say, giving into my laughter as I reach for her. Slipping under the comforter I find her hips, gripping and pulling her onto my lap. She yelps at the quick change of position, removing her face from her hands and wrapping her arms around my neck. The heat of her on my lap warms my body and I think of how easily I could slip out of my pants and into her in this position.

My face and hardening cock must give me away because she takes this opportunity to grind against me as she brings her mouth to the base of my neck. I groan as she sucks at the pulse point there, guiding her hips to move faster over me.

"We should make a plan for Christmas now," she says between kisses as her lips find their way to my jaw, sending shivers down my spine and straight to my cock.

"It's tomorrow," I argue, encouraging her to move faster and moving my hands up under the shirt she's wearing until the lace of her underwear is against my skin. The contrast of her smooth skin and the texture of the lace make me want to rip them off until I'm met with nothing but smoothness.

"Still, we're stuck here. You don't even have a tree," she argues, finally reaching my mouth and covering it with hers. I can taste the coffee when she slips her tongue into my mouth and my cock is begging to be surrounded by her again.

"Can you make a plan while I fuck you?" I ask, not wanting to wait another second. She's not going to settle before there's a plan, but I don't want us to get distracted afterward.

"Multitask? Sure, yeah, let's do that," she gasps, picking up her pace above me.

That's all the confirmation I need before I swipe the comforter on to the floor, laying her on the couch under me. Her shirt falls above her waist and I can see she's already soaked through her underwear. "You're already so wet for me, Vi," I say, dragging my finger from her entrance to her clit through her underwear, pushing with my thumb when I reach the spot that makes her lift her hips off the couch.

"Fuck, Noah," she gasps, and hearing my name on her lips fills my heart with so much pride and frustration that I've missed out on years of this. "Please fuck me," she mewls, arching further into my touch.

"Make your plan, and I will," I tease, moving off the couch and into the fort where there's a box of condoms. Reemerging with one in hand I stand next to the couch and slowly lose my sweatpants. "I don't hear any plans," I say as I settle on to the couch between her thighs.

"Right, plans," she nods, looking confused like she's unsure of what the word means. "First a tree. Do you have one hidden away?"

"No," I tell her, pumping myself once before opening and rolling the condom down my length. She watches me with hungry eyes, and I want to see how far she can get before she loses the ability to speak.

"Cat tree turned Christmas tree?" she asks through a gasp as I hook my fingers in her underwear and slide them down her legs.

"Sure, I think there's a box of ornaments somewhere," I tell her, kissing the top of her foot as I finish removing her underwear. I toss them to the floor and rest her ankle on my shoulder, opening her up and seeing where she's soaked and ready for me.

"Perfect. Food?" she asks, moving her hips up seeking the friction I haven't given her yet.

"I'll cook us a big breakfast today and tomorrow," I tell her, knowing I have plenty of breakfast food in my kitchen, and less dinner related items.

"Okay, presents?" She quickly moves on to the next thing as I lift her other leg and rest it on the back of the couch, moving forward and brushing the head of my cock along her center. She moans at the contact, throwing her head back and fully exposing the hickey that was partially hidden.

"What about..." I start, but trail off as I coat myself in her wetness and line the head of my cock at her entrance. Slowly pushing into her I continue as she writhes underneath me "...we find presents around here." I look down and see the head disappear into her and I'm already on the brink of collapse, but I don't want this to be over too fast. When she doesn't reply, I start to pull out.

She whines, and I tsk before she finds words. "That works. Please Noah," she begs.

Finally putting us out of our misery, I sink into her on the last syllable of my name, turning it into a scream. I drop and bracket my hands around her head, bringing the leg around my shoulder with me and folding her in half until my balls hit her heat.

We let out twin moans and I force myself to stay still inside her, soaking up the warmth and tightness around my cock.

"Anything else?" I ask, slowly pulling out of her, but not all the way.

"For what?" she fumbles over her words, her chest heaving. "Oh right, Christmas. Nope, that covers it," she rushes through the sentence as one hand moves her shirt up to her chin, exposing her breasts to the cool air and see they're already perfectly pebbled. "Now fuck me—oh fuck," she screams as I take one of her nipples into my mouth and thrust into her.

We don't waste any more time planning after that as I lose control when she lifts her hips to meet my thrusts. She's anything but quiet as I pick up the pace and kiss anywhere I can find bare skin. I want to mark every part of her body and erase anyone that's ever touched her before. I need to make up for the time we've lost, but I'm not sure anything will ever be enough.

When she reaches between us to touch her clit, her walls tighten around me as her orgasm rapidly approaches with mine not far behind it. I fuse her mouth with mine right when she comes apart, swallowing her moans and triggering my own release. I spill into the condom and slow down my thrusts as she works herself through her release, our heaving breathing the only sounds in the room.

I finally pull out of her and fall onto the couch. I might need food because I'm starting to feel lightheaded and I realize I haven't eaten much in the past twenty four hours.

"Breakfast?" she asks, standing and wobbling on her feet. I reach out to catch her, pulling her to my side and keeping her upright.

"Breakfast, but bathroom first," I agree, holding on to her as

I stand, not wanting to also wobble. I wrap her in my arms for one last kiss before leading us to the bathroom.

twenty-nine

NOAH

EVENTUALLY I LOST track of time after Christmas Eve morning, but spending several uninterrupted days with Violet was more than I could have hoped for. Unfortunately for Simon, we spent most of the week naked, making up for lost time. I think we lost power at one point, but I was too busy spending all my time wrapped up in her to notice. In turn, she took her time marking all my tattoos like I did to hers, as I learned what spots on her body elicited moans or giggles. We exchanged gifts on Christmas, me giving her several of my sweaters and her giving me a box of all the notes I had left her over the years. She found it in one of her boxes, and I almost cried when I saw them all together.

Yesterday, we finally managed to make it downstairs to bake the sugar cookies for the make-up event. All the stress I had from the previous month was nonexistent with Violet by my side. Between batches I managed to sneak a few orgasms in for her, which I wish I was doing right now. But seeing her beam like a shining star while surrounded by her family at the festival will have to do.

She's helping Ava decorate a sugar cookie as I stand off to

the side with Jacob and Iris. The family from the first night at the festival passes by and waves at me before grabbing cookies for themselves. It takes me a second to wave, because no one ever waves at me. It seems like the ending of the snowstorm must have put everyone in a good mood. We didn't end up winning the window decoration contest, but we've gotten multiple compliments on it and people seem excited for the shop to open.

"Did you ask her to stay?" Jacob nudges me, taking me out of my train of thought.

"Violet?" I ask, clarifying he didn't mean the woman I was waving to.

"Yes, who else would I be talking about?" He rolls his eyes.

"Shut up, Jacob. I told you not to ask unless Violet said anything first," Iris whisper-yells, hitting her husband in the arm.

"Well, too bad, I'm asking," he tells her, turning to me. "Did you ask her?"

"Do I have to?" I ask him, narrowing my eyes.

Jacob rolls his eyes again. "Take it from me, always ask. Even if she doesn't act like she wants you to, she does. Trust me," he finishes with finality nodding toward his wife.

Iris rolls her eyes, but the upturn of her mouth tells me he's probably been through something similar with her before.

I don't have time to reply before Ava comes running over with a cookie covered in frosting and sprinkles, Violet close behind her.

The second she's next to me, her hand finds mine and my heartbeat picks up slightly. No matter how many times I touch her I still get excited by that first touch. Jacob glances at our hands and then at me while Violet is distracted by a conversation with her sister.

Leaning closer to her, I whisper, "Take a walk with me?"

"Okay," she says. "We'll be right back." She turns to tell her family.

I lead her through the crowd to find a more private area to talk to her. I've floated around the idea of asking her to stay, but I've been too scared that she might say no. Part of me was hoping that I wouldn't have to ask, but that talk with Jacob confirms that I need to take that chance. It looks like it's going to have to wait another minute as I see Bernice approaching us.

She stops right in front of us, with the widest smile on her face. "It's so nice to see you two smiling together. I wanted to find you and apologize for any ill will I've sent your way. Thank you for donating the cookies for the contest. I'm looking forward to visiting the shop once you have it open," she tells me.

"Thank you," I stutter, not sure what else to say.

She nods, lips tight together in a thin line. Right as she's about to turn, Violet speaks from next to me.

"Also, I wanted to let you know Noah was never arrested. He was just helping a girl get away from a bar fight. And we'll set aside some cookies for you at the shop," she smiles, but her eyes say 'fuck you, Bernice' and I hold back a laugh at how proud I am to call this woman my other half.

"Good to know, enjoy the festival," she says quickly before disappearing into the crowd.

I glance over at Violet who is looking at me with the widest grin on her face. I don't understand what's in the air today to have everyone all of the sudden like me.

"That was weird, right? Her coming up to us?" I ask her.

"No. It was normal," she says, rolling her eyes at me. "That's what happens when people like you."

"Really?" I can't help but wonder if there could be another reason behind Bernice being so nice to me.

"Really. You've worked hard this last month. I'm so proud of you," she says, throwing her arms around my neck and pulling me closer to her. "Accept that people see you now. Plus now that she knows that you weren't arrested the whole town will know by the end of the day."

"Fine. And thank you," I reply, grabbing her face and kissing her quickly. "I did have a few things I wanted to talk to you about, actually."

"All good things I hope," she says, wrapping her arms around me and pulling me close.

"Of course. Now that the festival is over and I'm all set to open the shop, you don't really have a reason to keep hanging out there with me. But I was hoping, instead of going to your parents or the city, would you stay here with me?" I pause briefly to gauge her reaction, and see her eyes crinkle from how wide her lips have gone. "I want you to work with me. And move in with me. And never leave my side again in general, if that's okay with you?" I rush out the last part before I get ahead of myself and propose to her.

She squeals, jumping into my arms the best she can from our current position. I wrap my arms under her butt, allowing for her legs to meet behind my back. She starts kissing any part of skin that's not covered by some type of winter clothing, saying "yes, yes, yes" between each kiss. A small part of me hopes she's leaving behind red marks from her lipstick.

When her lips finally reach my mouth I cup her cheek and hold her close, tasting sugar cookies and the future.

epilogue

"FUCK!" I yell as a group of kids on bikes come flying off the sidewalk and onto the street.

"What now?" My sister's voice fills the car.

"Do some parents not teach their kids to look both ways before crossing the street?" I grumble, collecting myself before driving again.

"I don't know, everyone else does it wrong but us," Iris says. "Are you almost back?"

"Yeah, remind me why I'm the one who had to drive out of town to pick up this banner when you ordered it?" I sigh, annoyed we couldn't make a homemade banner for my parents' fiftieth wedding anniversary.

"Because I had to make sure the caterers know where to put everything. You're stopping by Gingerbreads to get the dessert right?" Iris asks, and I can hear her giving someone else directions on where to put the cheese and crackers.

"Yes, I'm almost there now. I'll be at your place soon. Do you need anything else?" I ask her one last time.

"Just your beautiful face, see you soon." She ends the call without a goodbye as I park on the street outside the shop.

The sign reads 'CLOSED' because of the party today, so I unlock the door with my keys. Walking in, I see boxes of cookies ready to go but no sign of my husband.

"Noah?" I call out, hoping he isn't upstairs.

A second later, his head pops out from the kitchen door. He's as handsome as always, with his dark frames and dark hair. He's rocking a full beard these days, although it's been trimmed for today. His plaid flannel is rolled up to show off his tattoos, and his dark jeans and boots are perfect for the early fall weather.

"Don't be mad," he says, playfulness in his voice. "I lost Lily."

I stifle my laugh, this is the third time he's 'lost' Lily this week. Getting into character, I step around him and through the kitchen door, giving him a small kiss on the cheek before loudly saying, "What do you mean you lost her? What happened?"

He grins at me, running his fingers through his hair like every other time before. "We were playing hide and seek and she's too good."

Suddenly, we hear a giggle from underneath the center table. I look at Noah with a tilt of my head, and he puts one finger over his mouth.

"I guess if I can't find her, she'll have to miss the party," he says loudly as I shake my head.

Right on cue, Lily springs out from under the table. "I'm right here, Daddy!"

He pretends to be shocked as she bounces into his arms, her dark pigtails swinging as he picks her up and spins her around. I'm thankful he was able to get her dressed in the red jumpsuit I bought for her the other week. Although, I can see he wasn't able to convince her to wear anything besides her yellow rain boots she hasn't parted with since April. I'm certain that she's going to ask us to turn them into winter boots by Christmas.

"Thank God we found you," I call out, moving to his side and tucking myself into his childfree arm. "We ready to get our party on?" I ask Lily, tickling her stomach and causing her to shriek and squirm in his arm.

"Let's go before this one hides on us again," he says, scrunching his face at Lily. She returns his look with an equally scrunched face and I can't believe I got this lucky.

Gingerbreads was officially reopened the day after Noah asked me to stay. On opening day, we ran out of cookies before lunch, and told everyone to come back in a few hours as we baked more. Everyone who stopped by talked about how they loved getting to eat them again at the festival, and they were all anticipating the opening. Bernice did her duty and spread the word that Noah hadn't actually gotten arrested, which helped people be more comfortable with him. That combined with how much he opened up after me and Simon, things really turned around.

After a week of having the shop open, all the teenagers who were forced to quit because of their parents were rehired. Their friends became regulars like Noah and I were in high school, and the store quickly became a place of laughter again. Seeing the look on Noah's face when people would come in to see him and ask about Simon or new flavors was priceless. Someone even asked for the peanut butter and jelly cookie that Ginger used to make, which Noah promised would be back soon.

It was easy to fall into a routine with him, him baking and me handling all the business aspects. We would work all day and find ourselves frantically rushing up the stairs to fall into bed. It seems like yesterday when he got down on one knee at the tree lighting and asked me to marry him. I didn't let him get the question out before I tackled him to the ground.

Then Lily came along almost three years ago, right in time for Christmas morning. Simon was obsessed with her the moment we came through the door with her. Now he never leaves her side.

We quickly outgrew the apartment upstairs, and found a small house close to Main Street. Now it's a space to relax or let Lily sleep while we work. Luckily the new house has three bedrooms. One for us, one for Lily, and one for the surprise I get to share with Noah tonight when we're home. I don't want to take the attention away from my parents, and I want a moment to celebrate with him alone.

I redirect my train of thought when Noah looks at me, worried he'll be able to read my mind. Fortunately, he doesn't and we head out of the shop with our copycat, her rain boots squeaking with every step.

A few hours later, Iris's house is packed with friends and family all here to celebrate my parents. She's been running around making sure all the food is being refilled, even though I told her it's literally the caterers job. Luckily, I haven't had much time to talk to her with all the tasks she keeps sending me on. When I found out I was pregnant with Lily she knew the moment I stepped into her house, which shot my whole announcement plan out the window.

I'm worried if I talk to her for too long today I'm going to spill the beans before I get the chance to tell Noah. I've successfully been able to ditch any alcoholic drinks he's given me, and no one noticed when I spit my champagne into my glass, all too focused on my parents. If I was to tell Noah I wasn't drinking he would know something was up, since I usually have one or two drinks at these types of events. He's also on Lily duty since I'm helping Iris host. He and Jacob have her and Ava distracted outside with the bouncy castle. Ava is one of Lily's favorite people, and I can hear her squeals of joy coming in through the open back door as I close my eyes and soak up the sounds around me.

"What are you doing?" Iris's voice makes me jump as she comes up out of nowhere and I drop the sparkling water I was pouring into an unlabeled plastic cup.

"Shit, Iris. Don't sneak up on me," I say, grabbing a handful of cocktail napkins to soak up the spilled water.

"Sorry, you were standing here for a minute, it was weird," she tells me, seeing the mess I've made on the drinks table. "Oh my god, are you pregnant?" she whisper-yells, stepping closer to me and picking up the can of sparkling water.

My mouth drops open and I'm speechless as she gasps and covers her mouth. I should have told Noah this morning and avoided her all day. If I ever get pregnant again I'm blocking her until I want to tell her.

"How the fuck?" is all I can manage, pulling her down the hall so no one else overhears us and posts about it on the town's Facebook page.

"You never drink sparkling water," she says, holding up the can. "So that means, you were pouring it into a cup so it looked bubbly like an alcoholic drink so no one knew you weren't drinking. There's no way you wouldn't drink at this; hell, I started drinking at eleven. A day filled with everyone in town? I need some assistance there."

"You should be a detective not an eye doctor," I laugh, grabbing the can from her hand and taking a sip. The fizziness of the water hits my tongue and I almost gag, water should never be bubbly and I remember why I hate this stuff.

"Vi, I'm so happy for you!" she shouts, pulling me into a quick hug before pushing me away. "Wait, does anyone know?"

I shake my head. "No, I was going to tell Noah after the party. I didn't want to distract from Mom and Dad's day," I tell her.

"Well that won't do, go grab him and take him upstairs. Jacob can watch Lily," Iris says, giving me no say in the matter when she takes my hand and drags me through the crowd of people to where our husbands and daughters are.

"Noah, can you help Violet grab something from upstairs?" she asks.

He clearly doesn't suspect anything when he spins around and follows me into the house and upstairs. He's going on about how Lily was trying to do flips in the bouncy castle, and maybe we should think about putting her into gymnastics so she doesn't hurt herself while my heart is acting like it's about to flip out of my chest. I don't understand why I'm so nervous to tell him. When I got pregnant with Lily he was so ecstatic, I don't see why he wouldn't be now. We weren't trying, but I never started taking birth control again after Lily and we ran out of condoms.

He's still talking when I pull him into Iris's spare room and shut the door behind me.

"What are we getting?" He looks around, confused when he doesn't see any boxes laying around.

"Actually, there's something I need to talk to you about," I say, trying to figure out how to tell him without blurting it out.

"Okay well now I'm worried. What's wrong?" He's standing in front of me in a flash, warm hands on my shoulders and traveling down my arms to intertwine his hands with mine.

"I'm pregnant," spills out of my mouth instead of the carefully crafted introduction and easing into I had been rehearsing for the last two minutes.

He doesn't say anything, he just scoops me in his arms and guides my legs around his body as he spins me around cheering.

The instant relief floods through my body and I throw my head back, letting my hair fly in the wind.

"When did you find out?" he asks, finally coming to a stop and keeping me tucked in his arms.

"This morning, right after you left and before I went to get the banner," I tell him.

"I'm so excited, Violet. I can't wait to raise another kid with you," he says through the widest smile, kissing me and holding me closer to him.

We stay like that for a bit longer, making out in a guest room like two teenagers before returning to the party.

When we get outside, Lily tumbles out of the bouncy castle and Noah catches her right before she smacks her head on the ground. Looking at the two of them as he scoops her in his arms fills my heart with so much joy, and I can't wait to grow our family more. I can't believe how lucky I am to have found a place where I truly belong.

THE END

Ready for the next book in the Evergreen Lake: Under the Mistletoe series? Check out *Hung by the Fire* by Shea Brighton.

evergreen lake

UNDER THE MISTLETOE

dicktionary

For anyone looking to know when open-door scenes occur. Including a solo scene, they can be found in the following chapters:

- Six
- Fifteen
- Twenty
- Twenty-Five
- Twenty-Seven
- Twenty-Eight

acknowledgments

To the authors in this holiday collection; Nicole Sanchez, Shea Brighton, Alexia Chase, Shana Gray, DL Gallie, Lynessa Layne, Rebecca Barber, and Rhian Cahill. I had a pleasure working on creating this world with all of you, I can't wait for readers to enter Evergreen Lake!

To the Evergreen Lake designer, Jordan, thank you for helping us make the holiday magic feel real with your amazing covers and map! You've been so much fun to work with and I can't wait to work on future projects with you!

To my alpha and beta readers, Lauren B., Nicole, Chelsea, Hannah, Lauren, Megan, Mellie, Paige, Paula, Rebecca, and Sophia. Thank you for taking the time to help me make this holiday story the best it could be! This story wouldn't be the same without you.

To my editor, Kristen, thank you for all the work you put into perfecting this book! This book wouldn't have gotten that extra finishing touch without you.

And lastly to you, the reader, thank you for picking up Violet & Noah's story. I hope you enjoyed reading it and remember to believe in yourself and take a chance!

about the author

Kayla Martin (she/her) lives in Upstate New York with her husband and Neptune—her tuxedo cat and writing assistant. As an avid reader and audiobook lover, Kayla loves to write swoon-worthy stories that will pull at your heartstrings. Using her big family as inspiration, there is no shortage of hijinks and family meddling involved in each character's story. She believes in writing love stories that help you find joy while also exploring different human experiences about sexuality, mental health, and everything in between.

Connect with Kayla on her website at www.kaylamartinauthor.com to sign up for her newsletter and get early access to news about her latest book! Find Kayla on the following platforms:

also by kayla martin

Murphy Family Series

A Thousand Sunsets: A shy recent college grad is looking forward to a calm family vacation until a game of twenty questions with the new tall, dark, and tattooed lifeguard goes further than either of them intended in this hot summer rom-com.

www.ingramcontent.com/pod-product-compliance
Lightning Source LLC
Chambersburg PA
CBHW070728230225
22232CB00006B/24